KULA

A Surfing Detective Mystery

Other Surfing Detective books
by Chip Hughes

MURDER ON MOLOKA'I

WIPEOUT!

SURFING DETECTIVE
CONFIDENTIAL INVESTIGATIONS · ALL ISLANDS

KULA

A Surfing Detective Mystery

CHIP HUGHES

SLATE RIDGE PRESS

SLATE RIDGE PRESS

P.O Box 1886
Kailua, HI 96734
slateridgepress@hawaii.rr.com

ISBN: 0982944438
ISBN-13: 9780982944431

First Edition, First Printing 2011

for Judy

I looked at the cast-off animals
and saw in their eyes love and hope, fear and dread,
sadness and betrayal.
I was angry.

"God," I said, "Why don't you do something?"
"I have," God replied. "I created you."

—*author unknown*

ACKNOWLEDGEMENTS

Many thanks once again to my wife, collaborator, and inspiration, Charlene Avallone; and to veteran Honolulu PI Stu Hilt. Specialist editors who assisted include Moke Strassberg president of the Golden Retriever Club of Hawai'i; Robert Sullivan, Anne Kennedy, and Roger Tansley, who checked Australian places and phrases; and Normie Salvador and Rodney Morales, who sharpened pidgin dialect. *Mahalo* to Josie Morgan of the Hawai'i Island Humane Society; and to Lorna and Shel Hershinow and Laurie Tomchak, for correcting my many mistakes. Thanks also to Suzanne McClure, Les Peetz, Raybern Freitas, Kirsten Whatley, Suzanne Kukana, and to CEO Dale Madden and Art Director Scott Kaneshiro at Island Heritage. I'm very grateful to Christine Matthews and Robert Randisi of the Private Eye Writers of America—an indispensable organization for writers of P.I. fiction. Warm aloha to my sister, Judy Michener, to whom this book is dedicated, my webmaster John Michener, and my niece April Stokes. Finally, thank you to Cissy Crosby and Donna Engelbardt for the cover photo of the Boomer (a.k.a. Kula), the golden retriever who inspired this book.

one

Friday morning, I'd barely opened my office window to the trade wind breeze when a knock rattled the door. Frank Fernandez's huge frame filled the doorway. The scowl on his face might have scared me if I hadn't known him better.

"Kai, I gotta ask you some questions," said the gravel-voiced homicide detective. His bloodshot eyes suggested he hadn't slept much the previous night.

Frank Fernandez and I had crossed paths before, working the same case from different angles. His linebacker bulk and macho vibe seldom failed to make bad guys tremble. Even with good guys Frank could be a grizzly bear or a teddy bear, depending on his mood. I hoped this morning he was feeling warm and cuddly.

"Fire away, Frank." I gestured to my client's chair and he wedged himself in. The spicy scent of his aftershave followed him down.

"Where were you last night after midnight?" He skipped the pleasantries.

"Home in bed," I said.

"Anybody with you?" He studied my face.

"The sad truth is, Frank, I slept alone."

"Can anyone verify that?"

"No."

"So you've got no alibi?"

"For what?" I disliked the direction he was going.

Fernandez uttered a man's name—the man I'd met in Waimānalo the night before. "He was found early this morning with a crushed skull. Two of his friends accuse you. They say you killed him last night, then you stole his shark-tooth necklace."

"I don't make empty threats," I said. "And why would I kill for a shark's tooth when I've already got sixteen of them etched on my chest?"

"Do you deny you drew your revolver on him?"

I stuffed my hands into my pockets and retreated behind my desk. "He and his Moke pals tried to steal my surfboard. I drew to scare them off, to save my board. I would never even have talked with the guy, but he said he had a tip for a case I'm working on. Besides, didn't you say his skull was bashed?"

"What case?" Frank asked, deflecting my question.

"A missing person. Nobody you know." I was getting agitated.

"That's not what I heard. I heard you're looking for a dog."

I glanced down at my feet. "OK . . . I'm looking for a dog, Frank. It's not an easy thing to admit."

"That's funny, Kai. Very funny." Fernandez sneered. "You've sunk to a new low."

"These aren't the best of times, Frank. Haven't you noticed?"

"Give me a break."

"I'm not on the city payroll like you. If I don't have cases, I don't get paid."

"But looking for lost dogs?"

"Well, maybe I like cold noses and warm hearts."

Fernandez laughed. "Next time I'll bring my violin."

No way would I tell the homicide detective who I was working for. The dog's master, that is. Client confidentiality is a matter of principle. Even in the case of murder, and even when the finger was pointing at me.

two

Fernandez was right. I had sunk to a new low.

I had arrived there four days earlier. The June sky was the milky sapphire of a Blue Hawaiian as my '69 Impala inhaled its last fumes of no-name gasoline, pinging and belching up to the summit of Tantalus Drive—a winding mountain road with breathtaking views of Honolulu. But it wasn't the views I found tantalizing on this Monday morning, so much as the visible wealth that lined the switchback drive in the form of sprawling mansions, exotic landscaping, and luxury cars.

I was heading for one of those mansions owned by Barry Buckingham—entrepreneur, yachtsman, and charismatic radio pitchman who sold precious metals, gold mostly, over the airwaves.

I knew Mr. Buckingham had his detractors. He'd been called a fraud, charlatan, huckster, and a few other choice names. The high cost of living in Hawai'i makes islanders vulnerable to get-rich-quick schemes. And if we lose, we can always find someone to blame. Buckingham was an easy target, despite testimonials to his moneymaking wizardry. It was also common knowledge that people feared him.

Since he was my only paying client on the horizon, I gave Barry Buckingham the benefit of the doubt. Was I skeptical? Sure. But I couldn't allow skepticism to come between me and a paycheck.

Surfing all day, every day, is nice work if you can get it. Even if I could afford to surf that much, there's something about having a case that keeps me going. And ever since I found that big-wave rider in upcountry Maui who everyone thought had drowned, I've had a thing for locating missing persons. So never mind my qualms about the pitchman, I was anxious to meet him.

Mr. Buckingham's wife had vanished four months earlier in February. The papers were full of stories about the odd disappearance of Cheyenne Sin. Honolulu police hadn't come up with anything, except to suspect Mr. Buckingham himself. So when he said he needed my services, I naturally assumed he meant to search for his wife and get himself removed from the suspect list.

Since I'd never met the man, I figured he found me in the yellow pages or on the internet. My ads show a longboard rider and say SURFING DETECTIVE: CONFIDENTIAL INVESTIGATIONS—ALL ISLANDS. For the record, I'm Kai Cooke. My first name means "sea" and my last comes from an old New England family. I'm thirty-four, single, and was *hānaied,* or adopted, by Hawaiian relations after my parents died when I was eight. I have sun-bleached brown hair and stand six feet even. Well, almost. At work I wear an aloha shirt, khakis, and sandals. At play I wear board shorts. I try to keep a balance between the two. Work and play, that is.

Neither the yellow pages nor my website had generated much business lately. Cases seemed as hard to catch as Waikīkī waves on a crowded Sunday afternoon. Two multi-state agencies—the PI equivalent of Walmart—had slammed their toll-free numbers and splashy ads next to mine. These agencies didn't have offices or overhead in Honolulu—just local hired guns—so they could undercut even my cheapest prices.

That's why I was climbing Tantalus to Buckingham's hilltop estate. He called it Wonderview. From up here you could see from Diamond Head all the way to Pearl Harbor—almost worth the eleven million my prospect had dropped on the place.

Standing alone outside the white privacy wall that surrounded the mansion, I felt even more broke than I was—like a guy down on his luck begging for a job. Not far from the truth. I wandered the wall until I found a path, blocked by a green copper gate decorated with dolphins. A few words into an intercom got me buzzed through.

Around the rambling white Mediterranean villa sprawled a tennis court, swimming pool and spa, and enough open lawn to host a *lūʻau* with several hundred guests. Whether or not Buckingham was on the up-and-up, it looked as if he could afford my services.

I climbed granite steps to a sweeping portico and stood in front of massive *koa* doors. I didn't have to knock. One swung open to a leggy teenager whose T-shirt displayed a windjammer at sea over the words Punahou Sailing Team. Her features were delicate, faintly Asian beneath carrot-colored hair. She did not greet me, just turned her back and shouted: "Daddy, he's here!" Then she left.

Taking this announcement for an invitation to enter, I crossed the marble threshold and waited.

The teenager returned with her father, a bigger, burlier man than I had imagined from his radio voice. It's rare to see anyone in the islands dressed like Buckingham was. I figured it was the custom down under, since he came from Australia. The gold dealer's charcoal double-breasted suit set off a cream-colored shirt and ruby tie that accentuated his ruddy complexion. Despite its elegance, his outfit looked ill-fitting on his meaty frame—shirt collar too tight, coat shoulders too broad—like of an overdressed gangster. To him, I must have looked underdressed in my aloha attire. Lucky he couldn't see my board shorts underneath.

His right hand reached out, gleaming with gold rings. One had a diamond the size of a walnut. But even the glint of that rock could not disguise the hugeness of his hand and the power of its grip—more like that of a sailor or butcher than a precious metals broker. I could see why people might be afraid of him. At the same time I could see why his smile had won over so many.

"G'day, Mr. Cooke," he announced in velvety Australian tones. "Welcome to Wonderview."

"Thank you, sir." I peered into eyes as pale blue as an empty sky. His black hair didn't match his complexion. Near his scalp I could see red roots.

"You know who *I* am, of course," he said with self-satisfaction. "And this is Lehua." The teenager nodded.

My celebrity host led me, his daughter trailing behind, into an enormous sunken living room. He gestured to the floor-to-ceiling glass where the morning sun streamed in. The ocean view took in the entire panorama of the south shore—from the cobalt green lochs of Pearl Harbor to the turquoise waves of Waikīkī. Those waves looked inviting. I hoped I could concentrate on what Mr. Buckingham was about to tell me.

I pulled my eyes away from the windows and checked out four Hawaiian quilts on the walls. They were hand-sewn in traditional patterns I recognized from living with the Kealohas, my adopted Hawaiian family. *'Ulu* or bread-fruit, *pua aloalo* or hibiscus, *hala kahiki* or pineapple, and *kukui* or candlenut tree. I was surprised how faded they were. You'd think someone who could afford such expensive pieces would take better care of them. At least keep them out of the sun. But Buckingham didn't seem to know what he had.

He pointed me to an overstuffed leather chair of white hide that must have inconvenienced one very big cow. He and his daughter took a matching sofa at a right angle to me. They sat close together. Not touching, but close. The girl glanced up into his eyes. Was she looking for reassurance? Comfort? Courage?

"Mr. Cooke, I rang you because we've had a heartbreaking loss."

"I'm so sorry about your wife, sir," I said, truly feeling for him, while secretly smug that I knew my client's needs even before he expressed them. Her disappearance had been on TV and in the papers, so it was hard to miss.

"Right. My wife, Cheyenne Sin, disappeared in February. Bloody awful! The police are looking, but have gotten nowhere. That's why I called you about this other matter. I want a proper investigation. A *discreet* investigation."

"What other matter, sir?"

"Yesterday at Kailua Beach Park where Lehua took him surfing, our beloved Kula disappeared. I believe he was pinched."

"Pinched?"

"Nicked." He gestured with his big hands. "Stolen."

"You mean kidnapped?" I asked, thinking he was telling me another family member had disappeared.

"You could say that." Buckingham pulled a starched white handkerchief from his breast pocket. "No worries, love." He dried his daughter's tears. "Mr. Cooke is going to find Kula," he told her.

"Kula is your brother?" I glanced at the teenager, who was now openly crying.

"No," she said through her tears—"my dog."

three

"Your *dog?*"

"Kula is a special dog, Mr. Cooke," Buckingham replied. "His name means 'gold' in Hawaiian, as I'm sure you know, and he's the most stunning retriever you'll ever see. A beautiful boy. Kula belonged to my wife."

Buckingham didn't strike me as the type to get sentimental about a pet—or even a wife. He did seem devoted to his daughter, though.

Lehua rose and picked up a photo album from the coffee table. She handed it to me. "This is Kula." She sighed and returned to the sofa.

I opened the book of photos. All of the dog.

Kula was not red or sandy-brown like most golden retrievers, but sunny blond. His mane and feathering were luminous. His blond lashes set off dark brown eyes. *Beautiful boy.* Even I could see that this was one stunning canine. Pedigree was written all over him. And his collar—tanned and stitched leather—was embossed in gold with his name.

"Nice-looking dog," I said. "But finding lost pets isn't my usual—"

"Kula is not just my wife's dog," Buckingham interrupted. "He's a surfing dog. And you, I understand, are the Surfing Detective?"

"Yes, but I'm not a dogcatcher."

"Take a look at this, mate." Buckingham walked to a mammoth flat-screen TV and slipped in a DVD. The screen lit up with the blond retriever careering down the face of a massive wave at Mākaha. The dog was crouched low on the nose of a longboard piloted by Lehua. The narrator from a local TV news show referred to Kula as the "famous Hawaiian surfing dog." I'd heard of dogs riding knee-high stuff, but never one who could handle a legendary big-wave venue like Mākaha. I had to admit I was impressed.

"So you can see," Buckingham said as the video ended, "why we called you."

"Yes, sir." I cleared my throat and swallowed my pride. "I'll need a retainer. One thousand up front to begin the investigation."

"You'll have the whole amount in cash before you leave."

"Thanks," I said. No surprise. Men like Buckingham carry more in their wallet than I carry in my bank account. "Now I have some questions for you." I reached for the small spiral-bound pad in the pocket of my aloha shirt and the pen clipped to it. "Do you suspect anyone of stealing your dog?"

"Our housecleaner spotted a prowler on the property not long before Kula went missing."

"What did he look like?"

"A slim, longhaired bloke. I told the police but, as usual, they came up with nothing."

"Why didn't he steal the dog here? Why go all the way across the island to Kailua Beach?" I asked.

"I don't know," Buckingham said. "Maybe he saw our security system and ran."

"Do you suspect anybody else?"

"A few of my neighbors wouldn't be above taking a dog to make a point. I heard Mrs. Gum, the old bat across the street, is going to sue me."

"What for?"

"She claims my palms block her view." Buckingham shook his head. "There's more frivolous litigation in this country . . ."

"An old lady—steal a dog?"

"She has an axe to grind, that's for sure."

"OK, I'll interview her. Anyone else?"

"Dr. Carreras, my neighbor down the hill. Used to be a psychiatrist. He's complained constantly about Kula's barking and he accuses me of damaging his bloody sports cars."

"How do you mean, damage his cars?"

"Oh, he collects vintage sports cars: Jaguar, Ferrari, Porsche. I'm a *Rolls man* myself." Buckingham winked. "Anyway, my swimming pool overflowed last winter and Carreras claimed the water leaked into his garage and harmed his precious heirlooms. I seriously doubt it, but he's a miserable bloke. Drives like the devil on these mountain roads. Going to kill somebody . . ."

"I'll talk with him too." I turned to Lehua. "Do you know of anyone who might want to take Kula? Or could he have just wandered off?"

"No way," Lehua insisted. "He always stays right with me. But after we paddled in from surfing at Flat Island that day, I turned around and he was gone. I looked everywhere."

"You didn't see anyone suspicious? No car speeding away? No prints in the sand?"

"No. He just wasn't there . . ." She wiped away a fresh tear.

Buckingham drew his daughter to his side and said to me softly, "Since her mother disappeared, Kula has been Lehua's only comfort. You can imagine how difficult this is for her."

"I understand, sir." I paused, then returned to my growing list of suspects. "And what about enemies? Anyone who might want to hurt you or your family?"

He shook his head. "I'm a public man. Thousands listen to my radio program daily. Crazy people are out there, alongside the sane ones."

"Any threats?"

"Of course, but not lately." He looked away. "Nothing that could pertain to this."

I wasn't entirely convinced. I turned again to the girl, who seemed deeply pained about the dog.

"I know Kula's disappearance must be hard for you, Lehua, but it's important that you tell me everything that happened that morning on Kailua Beach—even if it might seem unrelated to Kula."

Still tearful, she said, "I'll try."

"I'll leave you two to talk while I go fetch your retainer," said Buckingham. He left the room through two elaborately carved doors.

Standing there with the girl, who recounted in detail what she'd already told me, I still wondered why my client had hired me to search for his dog instead of his wife. I could have backed out . . . but I felt sorry for the kid. I had a dog once and lost him, so I could relate.

"Lehua, I'm going to do everything I can to find Kula."

"Thank you so much!" she said.

"I know how it feels when your dog doesn't come home one day. I know how it feels when he never comes home."

She sobbed.

"But that's not going to happen with your dog."

"I'm so sad." She leaned her tear-stained face against my chest.

"There . . . there." I patted her shoulder. "We're going to make it better. I promise."

I was about to tell her every step I would take to find Kula, when I realized I hadn't the foggiest idea where to start. I had never traced a missing pet before. And never thought I would. So I settled for . . .

"By tomorrow I'll be on Kula's trail. You can count on it."

"You'll find him," she said, looking hopeful. "I know you will."

I felt almost guilty when she said that. So now I had two reasons why I couldn't back out. The kid. And the money.

Soon the gold dealer returned with ten crisp hundreds. I took them without a second thought.

four

After leaving Wonderview I crossed Tantalus Drive to the *mauka,* or mountain, side of the street. The cream colonial sat high on an incline and appeared to command at least a partial view of my client's villa and grounds. Was this the home of the old lady who Buckingham said had an axe to grind? Had she been involved in a dog-napping I suspected Kula had just wandered off and was within a few blocks of Kailua Beach. But checking out the neighborhood would at least make it look like I was earning my fee.

I climbed the steep driveway to the colonial's door, then turned and looked back toward Buckingham's estate. Yes, his royal palms did, in fact, block what would have otherwise been a stunning ocean view. A few chinks of blue were visible through the fronds, and beneath them a piece of my client's sprawling grounds.

I knocked and the door opened immediately, as if the occupant was expecting me. A rail-thin, silver-haired Chinese lady scoured me from my sandals to my sun-bleached hair. She was either very suspicious or very curious.

"Sorry to trouble you," I said and handed her my card. "I'm investigating the disappearance of your neighbor's dog." She glanced at my card. "Well . . . I'm Mrs. Gum. Maybe you heard of Gum's?" Her eyes searched my face, as she switched to pidgin. "Was my husband's appliance store on McCully. He wen die t'ree years ago. Now I take care dis whole place all by myself."

"Yeah, I know your husband's store," I said, switching to pidgin too. "Long time ago I buy one microwave ovah dere. Good deal. Stay working fine." Gum's was a humble mom-and-pop shop, which obviously hauled in oodles of cash to underwrite a home like this one on Tantalus Drive.

Mrs. Gum's face glowed. She was proud of her late husband's business.

I proceeded with my questions about the missing retriever, but she had not seen Kula lately, though she had noticed the absence of his bark that very morning. Which reminded me of another possible suspect, Dr. Carreras. I asked if her neighbor down the hill had ever complained to her about Kula. She said she hardly knew the doctor. Nor had she seen the prowler that Buckingham believed was haunting his home.

A high-pitched car horn blasted behind us. I turned to see a ruby-colored Rolls Royce gliding down Tantalus. The sun glinted on the silver figurine perched on its long hood—the "Flying Lady." The gigantic, glitzy machine seemed to huff: "I'm rich and powerful and could squash you like a bug!"

The driver waved. *Buckingham.* I remembered him saying, "I'm a *Rolls man*." As his mammoth car descended, I caught a glimpse of its vanity plate: GLD DLR.

Mrs. Gum's smile straightened. She nodded toward where Buckingham's car had been and whispered, "He did 'em."

"Mr. Buckingham stole his own dog?"

"No." Her whisper dropped a register. "He *make* his wife."

"Murdered his wife?" I tried to imagine it.

Mrs. Gum nodded. "Da police know. Dey jus no can prove 'em. I hear her screaming da night before she disappear. He wen kill her alright. But dey nevah going find her."

"You don't much like Mr. Buckingham," I said, beginning to think she was touched. "His palms block your view, right? That must make you mad."

She shrugged. Just then a dog barked somewhere, an octave too high for a big retriever.

"If I see da dog," she said, "I call you." With that, she shut the door.

I stood there, trying to wrap my brain around her accusation. If I didn't have my doubts about my client before, Mrs. Gum had planted the seeds. Or was she just spreading rumors about a neighbor she hated?

I began hiking down her driveway. When I glanced back, I saw the curtains part in an upstairs window and a face staring down at me. From where I stood, it was hard to tell whether it was a man or a woman. Despite what she told me, did the widow share her home with someone?

Or was I just imagining this, trying to turn the runaway dog into a real case?

five

Driving down the hill I spotted that south swell in Waikīkī I'd seen from Buckingham's living room. But I should have been watching my rear view mirror. Closing in on me from behind—too fast—was a yellow car. I could hear its motor revving. The car grew larger and larger in my mirror—on a collision course with my Impala. I stomped the accelerator, but before my V8 responded, the car—an older Porsche—swerved around me, tires squealing, and flew by.

"Maniac!" I yelled out the window as the Porsche passed at breakneck speed. All I could see of the driver was his silver hair.

I kept my foot on the pedal, trying to catch him. It would have been hopeless if the driver hadn't cut a ninety-degree turn into a side street and disappeared. When I reached the street I turned in too.

Down at the end of the short block the Porsche was parked in front of a four-car garage attached to a posh house nestled against the slope of Tantalus. In the open bays of the garage were three other vintage sports cars: a Jaguar in British racing green, a flame-red Ferrari, and a sapphire Morgan. The three were parked in perfect parallel formation, facing the open doors. Ready to roar. The Porsche's back hatch was open and the silver-haired driver walked toward it holding a wrench.

"You almost hit me back there!" I said as I got out of my car, wondering if he would hurl his wrench at me. Heat vapor rose from the back of the Porsche. The insignia on the engine hatch said 911S.

"Truly sorry," he said, placing his tool over his heart in a gesture of apology. He was a wiry man with an olive complexion and steel-gray mustache. "I just replaced the six carbs and they're giving me fits. These early air-cooled nine-elevens can be a bear to tune."

"Maybe you should save your testing for the track," I said. "Tantalus' hairpin turns aren't meant for speed."

"O'ahu's track closed," he said. "It was the only one on the island, and now it's gone. While politicians and racers argue about it, I make do. Anyway, I never drive beyond my abilities, or what conditions allow."

Having just seen him in action, I wondered.

"Max Carreras." He smiled and offered his hand. "I am sorry, honestly."

"Dr. Carreras?" I asked. "Just the man I wanted to see. I'm Kai Cooke." I handed him my card. Then I mentioned my client.

"You work for *him?*" Dr. Carreras said. "I might have to change my favorable impression of you."

"It's a long story," I said. Then I broached the subject of Buckingham's leaking swimming pool.

"Leak?" Dr. Carreras's olive complexion darkened, his gray mustache twitched. "Buckingham's pool *flooded* my garage. And the water carried a chemical that attacked the tires and wheels of my cars."

"Really?"

"See that E-Type?" He pointed to the low-slung green Jag in one of the bays. "The tires molded and the wire wheels started to pit. It took a helluva lot of work, I'll tell you, to bring them back."

"But you did, sir. They look beautiful—like brand new." I wasn't just saying that. They did look like new.

"To replace them with factory originals would have cost a small fortune. Buckingham nearly ruined all four tires and rims, and the rubber on my Porsche too." He paused. "So are you investigating the damage to my cars?"

"No, sir, I'm here about his dog. You complained to Mr. Buckingham about Kula barking?"

"Yes, I complained. And Buckingham did nothing. But since when did they start sending out PIs to deal with barking dogs?"

"The golden retriever is missing, sir, and I wondered—"

"Am I a suspect?"

"Well, I take it you don't care much for Kula?" I answered with a question of my own.

Dr. Carreras glanced at the heat vapor still rising from his Porsche. "The dog's a barker, but his master's the real problem."

"You and Mr. Buckingham don't get along?" I tried to keep him talking.

The doctor glanced up. "I've studied his type, Kai, my friend. Barry Buckingham is a phony. His business is built on empty promises and his hilltop mansion is mortgaged to the hilt. He's a fake."

"You really think so?"

"Take my advice," he said. "Collect your pay before he goes under."

"But—"

"Maybe we can continue this conversation later." The doctor bent down and began adjusting his new carburetors. "I could go on about Buckingham, but I've got to fit in another test drive before the rain comes."

"How about tomorrow?" I asked.

"Sure. But after you hear me out you won't want to work for him."

"I'll take that chance," I said. "Until tomorrow—drive safely."

"I never drive beyond my abilities," he said again. "Sorry if I gave you a scare, Kai."

"All in a day's work." I walked back to my car.

six

I pulled away from Dr. Carreras' four-bay garage with one thing on my mind—the surf. Turning onto Tantalus Drive I was surprised to see a gray cloud forming at the summit of the mountain. Was this the storm the doctor had predicted?

Leaving his stable of shining steeds behind, I couldn't help wondering about Dr. Carreras. While he appeared to take risks behind the wheel, I doubted he would be quite so reckless in other aspects of his life. A rich doctor had too much to lose if he got caught stealing a dog. Even if he was retired. Besides I found myself actually liking the man. Never mind he almost ran me off the road. I looked forward to talking to him the next day about my new client.

The doctor calling Buckingham a fake, right after Mrs. Gum's accusation of murder, shook my already shaky confidence in him. I needed time to think.

Surfing usually gives me what I need. When I'm out in the waves, my cares seem to drift away. What's back on shore can't touch me. I feel free. My head clears and I see things in a new way. That's how surfing helps me solve cases. Sherlock Holmes had his pipe—I have my surfboard.

* * *

Cunha's is a rare outside break—meaning the waves break far offshore—a few hundred yards out from the Kapahulu Avenue jetty and Prince Kūhio Beach Park in Waikīkī. The name of the surfing spot comes from an estate on the beach in the early 1900s owned by Emanuel Sylvester Cunha. Legend has it that Cunha built so close to the water that surf hitting the seawall splashed onto his *lānai*. It takes a large south swell to produce a rideable wave at Cunha's. Generally this only happens when summer storms kick up in the South Pacific. And even then, when Cunha's does break, you might wait half an hour for a ride.

But the wait is worth it. When you ride one of these sweeping rollers, you feel on top of the world. And while the long stretch between sets keeps the crowds down, it also allows plenty of time for reflective types to solve the world's problems and for a detective to sort out the details of his cases.

Cunha's surfers are patient surfers. Patience was what I needed. I, who know next to nothing about locating missing pets, had taken a case to find one. And I had taken it from a client about whom I had my doubts. I wasn't ready to buy into all the suspicions surrounding Buckingham, but I did wonder what I'd got myself into. So I paddled into the lineup and waited for a wave and an inspiration.

At Cunha's, waves form slowly and you must paddle hard to catch them. But once you're on, the tempo quickens and the curl turns sheer. I watched and waited for several minutes. Then I got lucky.

Out on the horizon a swell was coming. It looked like only a ripple in the distance, but as it approached it grew larger.

Soon I could see several waves forming. I started paddling well before the first wave in the set peaked. By the time it caught up with me, I was moving as fast as it was. I dropped in. The wave suddenly jacked up and I shot down the green wall, cutting a foamy trail behind me. *Ho, brah!*

After carving my last turn, I paddled back into the lineup hooting and smiling—but still waiting for that inspiration. I took several more rides to get it.

* * *

After surfing I called Buckingham and gave him an edited version of my interviews with his two neighbors. I didn't tell him about Mrs. Gum's accusation, but I did hint at Dr. Carreras's less than flattering remarks.

"Carreras?" Buckingham groused. "For a psychiatrist, he's a bloody poor judge of character."

I hoped my client was right.

seven

That night I had dinner with my attorney friend, Tommy Woo. Tommy, thanks to Cunha's, was my inspiration.

Tommy Woo had two cats, both strays, that had wandered into his life—a tabby who he claimed liked listening to Miles Davis, and a rag doll who preferred Charlie Parker. That's what he called them: Miles and Charlie, even though the rag doll was a girl. Tommy, who lived alone after two nasty divorces, had been smitten. Then one day Miles disappeared and Tommy was beside himself. He searched for days. Finally he stopped mentioning the tabby. Had he found him? And, if so, how?

When I arrived a little before seven at the dinky chop suey house on River Street, Ah Fook was packed. I put my name in for a party of two, joined the line outside, and waited for Tommy.

Ah Fook reeked with the ambience of this notorious backwater of Chinatown, where gamblers, smugglers, pimps, murderers, and thieves once plied their trades, and where legendary HPD Detective Chang Apana—prototype for the fictional Charlie Chan—hauled them in with his whip.

The savory smells of steamed clams, dim sum and Peking duck escaped as the door opened and closed, reminding me I hadn't eaten after my session at Cunha's. Despite run-ins with the health department and liquor commission, Ah Fook could always be counted on for a good, cheap meal. And if Tommy and I had anything in common, it was this: we were both cheap.

Soon a waitress waved me in and seated me in a dim corner. I looked around. Still no Tommy. He was late again. I began to wonder if my inspiration had tricked me. Sure my *akamai*—meaning smart—attorney friend could dazzle a jury with his eloquence, wow an audience with his jazz piano, and tell off-color jokes until your face turned blue. But find a missing pet? My fingers were crossed.

As the waitress returned with two cups and a steaming tea-pot, the door swung open to the familiar loose-jointed, lanky figure dressed all in black—looking like a parish priest of Chinatown. He saw me from across the room, tapped his wrist-watch, and mouthed: "Broken." We both knew he was lying. Attorney by day and a musician by night, Tommy Woo had a shaky relationship with time.

I poured tea, we both ordered the $8.95 dinner special, and then I got right to the point: "Tommy, what do you know about finding lost dogs?"

"Dogs?" He adjusted his tortoiseshell glasses, brushed back his gray hair, and let his first joke fly. "Did you hear the one about the three-legged Dalmatian and the sexy French poodle?"

"Many times." I lied.

Tommy looked stunned. He raised his brows and said nothing. A rare moment. The waitress came by and ladled egg drop soup into our bowls.

"I asked because a friend of mine needs help finding one." I bent the truth a little. "The dog is special. A golden retriever who rides a surfboard."

"What's his name?" Tommy sipped the hot soup.

"Kula."

"Not the dog," Tommy said. "The owner."

"Oh . . ." I paused, savoring my own soup. "Buckingham," I finally said.

"Barry Buckingham, the gold dealer?" Tommy asked, his expression returning to its usual animation. "Didn't know you knew him."

"I don't, really."

"So it's a case?" Tommy asked as our sweet-and-sour spare-ribs arrived. He picked up a rib and chewed on it. "Buckingham *hired* you to find his dog?"

"Right." I smothered the word in a mouthful of fried rice.

The stage was set for another of Tommy's doozies. He set down the rib, wiped the sauce from his lips, and placed his napkin back in his lap. "How can I help you?" he asked, without a hint of sarcasm. Sometimes Tommy surprised me.

"I remembered you lost that cat of yours, Miles? Did you ever find him?"

"He came home on his own," Tommy said, brushing back his hair again. "One morning I opened the door and Miles was sleeping on my doormat."

"Too bad."

"Too bad?"

"I mean that's good you found him. I was just hoping you'd tell me *how* you found him."

"I got lucky. But next time I'd call Maile."

"I knew a Maile once," I said. "What's her last name?"

"Barnes," he said. "Maile Barnes, the pet detective."

"Doesn't ring a bell. Pet detective, huh?" Was this another one of Tommy's jokes? "Like in an *Ace Ventura* movie?" I played along.

"No, she's for real. And she's the best—a former K-9 cop who finds lost animals."

The lemon chicken arrived and Tommy helped himself then passed the plate. He filled me in on Maile Barnes. Missing pet cases and now pet detectives. I was really hitting bottom.

"You should get a pet, Kai," Tommy added as he worked on his chicken. "You know, a dog or cat, so you're not alone so much."

"I don't have time for pets. Plus, the Edgewater doesn't allow them."

"Sneak one in."

"Then I'd have to feed it and walk it and pick up after it. I had a dog once, when my parents were still alive. So I know the drill."

Tommy adjusted his glasses and cocked his head. "We inhabit a lonely planet, Kai. Grab some comfort where you can."

"I do."

"You sure?"

Suddenly I felt irritated. "What makes you think I'm lonely?"

"Well . . . " He looked into my eyes. "Are you still hanging out with that Highcamp woman?"

I hesitated. "What if I am?"

Tommy kept looking at me. He said nothing.

"I gotta go." I got up and tossed a ten on the table. I didn't wait for my fortune cookie. It was bad enough that I'd been reduced to hunting missing animals; I didn't need any reminder of the dismal state of my love life.

"Phone Maile," Tommy called after me as I reached the door. I shook my head and walked out onto River Street. *What business is it of Tommy Woo who I hang out with?*

As I walked up the lamp-lit sidewalk, I cooled off a little and considered Tommy's suggestion.

eight

Tuesday morning's *Star-Advertiser* carried the following story in the "Hawai'i" section:

Fatal Crash on Tantalus

A 68-year old retired psychiatrist died yesterday as a result of injuries suffered in a one-car accident on Tantalus Drive at approximately 5 pm. The 1973 Porsche driven by Dr. Maxwell V. Carreras was traveling at a high rate of speed on upper Tantalus when it failed to negotiate a hairpin turn, slid down an embankment, and struck a tree. Rain-slick pavement from showers earlier in the day may have been a factor in the accident. Dr. Carreras was taken to Straub Clinic and Hospital in critical condition with head injuries and a collapsed lung. He was later pronounced dead at the hospital.

> There were no eyewitnesses to the fatal crash, but residents in the area said they heard the Porsche's engine, screeching tires, and then the collision. One resident who wished not to be identified said she thought she heard a second car also traveling at a high rate of speed, as if racing with Dr. Carreras' car. HPD closed off upper Tantalus Drive for several hours on Monday evening while their investigation was in progress . . .

The story went on, mentioning Dr. Carreras's loved ones left behind, his former medical practice, his hobby of collecting exotic cars, and so on. I had met him for the first time only yesterday, talked briefly about his neighbor, my client, and now the doctor was dead. I may have been one of the last people to see him alive. I recalled him saying that he never drove beyond his abilities, or what conditions allowed. He sounded so sure of himself. But now I had to conclude that he had been kidding himself about his abilities, or about those sharp turns on Tantalus Drive. But I couldn't picture him racing another motorist on that narrow mountain road.

Dr. Carreras's untimely death didn't sit well with me. I had actually liked the man. And I wondered, had the doctor survived, what more he might have told me about Buckingham.

* * *

Later that morning I drove to Mānoa, a mist-swept valley a few miles *mauka* of Waikīkī that lay between two ridges in the Koʻolau Range. I liked to hike to majestic Mānoa Falls, the deepest point in the valley, and trek along the stream that meanders from the falls and down past the Chinese cemetery to the floor below. I'd been coming to Mānoa since I was a student at Punahou, before my parents died. But today my destination was a cottage perched on a wooded slope on the eastern side of the valley, in line with the cemetery and about a mile from the falls. It was the home of pet detective Maile Barnes.

When I pulled up to the cottage it looked vaguely familiar. I felt like I'd been here before. *Déjà vu*. But I couldn't recall why or when.

I knocked and the door opened to a youthful brown-haired woman in Nikes, running shorts, and a sports bra. Tiny beads of sweat dotted her flushed cheeks and tanned limbs. Suddenly I knew why the place looked familiar. The years had treated her kindly. She appeared to be barely thirty, but I knew exactly how old she was.

"Maile Ohara," I said. "It's been a while. How are you?"

"I'm fine, Kai," she said. "But it's Barnes. My name hasn't been Ohara for years. You were away on the mainland too long."

"I was," I said, "and I regret it." She was wearing a ring, so I assumed Barnes was her married name. But it was not the name I expected.

"What ever happened to Karl?" I asked. "Weren't you two engaged senior year?"

"Long story," she said. "C'mon in, Kai, and tell me what you've been up to."

"I haven't been up to much," I said as we walked into a cozy island-style living room with rattan furniture on Oriental rugs. Open jalousies admitted a balmy breeze.

"Actually Tommy had lots to say about you." Maile gave me a knowing look.

"Don't believe a word," I said, gazing into her almond-colored eyes, a shade darker than her hair. I remembered her eyes and her skin too—fragrant and tawny like the loam of the Hawaiian soil.

"Tommy told me only good things," she said. "You can fill me in on the bad."

Maile and I went way back, though we hadn't seen each other since high school. We were born the same year in the same hospital—Queens—and were classmates at the same school—Punahou. I left Punahou, and later the islands, when Maile and I were in Mrs. Fegerstrom's third grade class. During the summer before my senior year at Flintridge Prep in La Cañada, California, I returned to O'ahu and reunited with my Punahou friends. Maile was a heartbreakingly beautiful seventeen year old then, who was dating a football star named Karl Knudson. There was still a comfortable closeness between Maile and me. I was drawn to her that summer, but Karl was never far away. She and I exchanged letters when I returned to California. We didn't write much after she became engaged.

"So what happened to Karl?" I asked.

"He played football at Stanford. He's a stockbroker in Modesto now with a wife and three kids."

"Why didn't you marry him?"

"I sent you a letter about it, but I didn't hear back from you."

"What letter? I never got it." I recalled that when I first moved to San Diego for college some of my mail got lost.

"I told you in the letter," Maile said. "My father got Parkinson's disease during my senior year. He was already in his sixties then. My mother tried to take care of him alone, but she wasn't young either. I couldn't leave them. Karl understood. We broke it off. In hindsight, it was for the best. I'm an Island girl. Can you imagine me in Modesto?"

I shook my head.

"What about you, Kai? Are you married? Do you have children?"

"No and no," I said. "I guess I've been too busy."

"Maybe you just haven't met the right person at the right time," Maile said. "Timing is everything. Karl and I——" She stopped in mid-sentence.

"But your timing must have been right later on," I said. "Who's the lucky Mr. Barnes?"

"Not so lucky, I'm afraid." Maile looked down. "Nestor was an HPD beat cop when I worked in K9. He fell in the line of duty."

"I had no idea." I was mortified. "I'm sorry."

"You had no way of knowing."

"I should have. I guess I've been out of touch."

"Stop scolding yourself and tell me about your missing dog."

I handed her Kula's photo. "I have to warn you—the last person I interviewed for this case died the same day."

Maile's eyes lit up when she saw the photo of the sunny retriever. "He's a beauty! What's his name?" She didn't ask about the dead man. A former cop, she took things in stride, I guessed.

"Kula. He's a famous surfing dog."

"I've heard of him," she said. "Wasn't he on TV?"

I nodded. She stepped to an antique roll-top desk and returned with a handful of cards.

MAILE BARNES

TRACER OF MISSING PETS

15 YEARS EXPERIENCE • K9 UNIT, H.P.D.

"Please pass them around," she said. "I always appreciate referrals."

I flipped the card over. Printed was her phone number, email address, and PO box.

"I'll be right back." She walked down the hall.

I looked around the room. Curled up on nearby rattan chairs were three contented cats. Maile soon returned in Bermudas and a tank top. She settled into a rattan loveseat opposite me and introduced her cats. "This is Coconut, a Siamese; Peppah, an Angora; and Lolo, a feral tri-color calico I'm trying to domesticate."

Judging from their looks, they had no cares in the world. The calico suddenly shot from the room when I reached for her.

"Don't mind Lolo. She's shy."

"No problem," I said. "Is she the reason you don't have a dog?"

"I used to—a German shepherd." She paused. "Rusty. He got on great with the cats, but . . ." She grew silent for a moment. "So, about your golden retriever—Kula." She uttered his name familiarly as if he were her own.

"He belongs to a Tantalus resident named Buckingham," I said. "Actually, he belongs to Mr. Buckingham's wife, Cheyenne Sin. She's missing too."

"Your client seems to be having a string of bad luck," Maile said.

"Yeah, so is his neighbor," I replied, thinking of Dr. Carreras. I shook my head. "Frankly, I don't know where to start. Then again, this is my first pet case. That's why I came to you."

Maile held Kula's photo close and studied it. "When I lost Rusty last year I searched all over Oʻahu. I would have found him if he were here. But I believe he was stolen and shipped off the island. It happens—more than you'd think."

"My client is convinced his dog was stolen."

Maile put her hands together as if in prayer. Her almond eyes rested on me. "I'd like to help you, Kai, but I'm leaving tonight for a pet refuge workshop in Utah. I won't be back until Sunday. You can't wait that long. Every day Kula is missing decreases the chances he'll be found."

Not what I wanted to hear. She saw my discouraged look.

"Tell you what," Maile said, "I'll give you a crash course in pet detection. Do you have the time now?"

"I'll make the time."

"Good." She stood up and disappeared again, this time into her galley-like kitchen.

Left alone, I scanned a gallery of photos on the far wall of the room: Her late husband in uniform, a dark and handsome local man; Maile in police blues holding a rifle and a medal inscribed "Expert"; several photos of a rust and black German shepherd.

Maile returned with two tall glasses of iced tea and a plate of cookies. I sipped the mint tea and bit in to a chewy cookie whose sweet, tropical aroma reminded me of my mother. "*Mmmmmm . . .*"

"Coconut," Maile said. "For old time's sake. When Tommy said you were coming . . ." She trailed off, seeming embarrassed.

There was an uncomfortable silence.

"Your husband was a handsome man." I pointed to his photo on the wall. "And I noticed one of you with a marksmanship medal."

She glanced over at the photos. "Nestor liked to target shoot and I tagged along. I have good eyes and a steady hand. Straight shooting came easy. In fact, the department once offered to reassign me from the K-9 unit to the SWAT team. But I didn't want to leave my dogs. Anyway," she glanced down, "that's all in the past."

"I'm sorry about your husband."

Maile looked up again. "Thank you, Kai. Now let's talk about your missing retriever . . ."

nine

"When a pet disappears," Maile explained, "every minute it wanders, its life is ticking away. The chances of it being hit by a car or euthanized in an animal shelter are high. That's why you have to work fast."

"Even if Kula was stolen?" I took another sip of mint tea.

"The sooner you're on his trail, the better. A beautiful pure-bred like Kula, even without papers, could bring top dollar. In Hawai'i, dogs are stolen for various reasons: resale, breeding, hunting, fighting. Fortunately, a golden retriever is not the kind of dog people here eat."

"Let's hope not." Growing up in the islands I'd heard stories about *poi* dogs, or mixed breeds, being eaten by certain groups. But it was hard to imagine anyone making a meal of such an expensive canine as Kula. And I'd given little thought to the fact that dogs were stolen for other purposes. I'd known people are kidnapped and possessions get stolen, but I never considered that anyone might filch the family pet. Maile had my attention.

"Theft by a puppy mill," she went on, "is a definite possibility. Kula would be a gold mine as a stud dog." She paused. "I fully believe there's an organized pet theft ring in the islands—some people discount it, but there's plenty of evidence."

"So you're telling me there's enough money to be made from walking off with man's best friend to encourage organized crime?" I must not have kept the doubt out of my voice, for she sounded slightly defensive when she replied.

"Small-time, maybe," she said, "but organized all the same." From beneath the rattan coffee table she drew a scrapbook. "I started collecting these clippings after Rusty disappeared."

"We have the same hobby," I said.

She looked at me funny.

"Clippings," I said. "Mine are about big-wave wipeouts and shark attacks."

She opened her book to a random page. "Here."

KAILUA DOG THEFTS REPORTED

Kailua residents are reporting that someone is stealing expensive, purebred dogs from their homes. "Six dogs were reported stolen in the past two months," said Charlene Nogata, manager of Windward Pets in Kailua. "One dog was apparently stolen from a kennel in a front yard," she added. Police have received numerous complaints about missing dogs in Kailua, and are looking into them. Nogata became alarmed when several dog owners visited her store and asked her to watch for anyone selling their pets. Stolen were a pair of Labrador puppies, a Jack Russell terrier, an Airedale, and two golden retrievers, dogs that can fetch $500 each, without registration papers. The store manager commented: "I've heard of individual owners losing their dogs, but never so many at once."

You'd think someone in my line of work might have taken more notice of such news. But then my business had always run more to the two-footed variety. Until now.

"Look at this." Maile turned the page to a notice in the "Pets for Sale" classifieds:

ATTN VETS & TECHNICIANS

Stolen from Pet's Haven on Beretania Street, Female King Charles Cavalier Spaniel. Microchip #500E239193. Reward for info. leading to arrest & conviction.

"Pet theft from a pet store? And a dog with an ID chip? That's bold."

"After being in law enforcement for fifteen years, Kai, I can tell you that some of the most twisted individuals I've run into are those who steal and mistreat animals. They're a sick bunch."

She turned another page.

DAD-GUM DOGNAPPERS!

Some people consider dogs fair game, just like mangoes in the yard. There's money to be made on stolen purebreds in the islands . . .

Page after page of clippings made a fairly convincing case for organized pet theft. Maile told me her role as a pet detective wasn't always an easy one. She had been cursed at, threatened, spit on, and even assaulted in her mission to rescue stolen animals. Once Maile had jumped from a window into a client's waiting pickup truck, clutching a Chihuahua after subduing the ex-husband with pepper spray. She had always had a tough side, even as a kid. But I hoped rescuing Kula wouldn't prove to be quite so dramatic.

Maile offered me some tips that would help whether he was lost or stolen: visit animal shelters, stake out and post signs where he was last seen, put ads in local newspapers, offer a substantial reward—the list went on. Before long I felt deeply in her debt.

"How can I ever thank you?" I asked.

"Could you drive me to the airport tonight? My ride fell through."

"I'd be happy to."

"And," Maile paused, "how would you feel about feeding Coconut, Peppah, and Lolo while I'm gone? Mrs. Kaneshiro, my next-door neighbor, usually does it, but she just got called to Kauaʻi to care for her sick sister. I was about to make some last-minute calls, but since you stopped by today and since we're old friends with a shared passion for animals . . ."

"Well . . ." Whatever had I said or done to make her think I was an animal lover?

Maile saw the doubt on my face. "I wouldn't normally ask anyone on such short notice, but I know I can trust you, Kai. I've always felt comfortable with you. And I'm sure my cats will too. So what do you say?"

I was flattered, but her little speech made me feel completely surrounded. There was really no way out. So I said, "Your three kitties and I should get along just fine."

"This is so nice of you!" She hugged me.

Her sweet, loamy fragrance made me almost glad I'd agreed and reminded me of that summer long ago when I had yearned for her.

"I'll show you how to feed and water them tonight before we go to the airport." Maile released me. "And I'll give you my cell number in case you have questions."

"Happy to help."

My agency on the brink, my only paying gig searching for a lost dog, and now I had become the reluctant butler to three pampered cats. How low I'd sunk!

ten

Early Wednesday morning before dawn I staked out Kailua Beach. Maile had suggested I start at five. Lost and frightened animals, she explained, sometimes return early in the morning to the place where they last saw their master. I sat in my Impala sipping Kona coffee and scanning the shore.

The two-mile crescent of Kailua Beach—a white ribbon dotted with palms—was barely visible in the grayness. My eyes kept returning to the decoy I had planted on the sand by the Lanikai boat ramp, at the exact spot where Lehua had last seen Kula. It was her beach cover-up and contained her scent; though undetectable to me, it would be as strong as perfume to the sensitive nose of a retriever.

Lehua had carried her surfboard onto the beach after riding waves with the dog at Flat Island—*Popoiʻa* or "fish rot" in Hawaiian—a small coral islet and seabird sanctuary about a quarter mile off shore. When she turned around, Kula was gone.

The sky began to lighten. There was still no one on the beach. I switched on the dome light and scanned the morning's *Star-Advertiser*. I flipped first to the obituaries. None yet for Dr. Carreras. I found myself thinking about him—retired psychiatrist, collector of vintage sports cars, Tantalus resident, and neighbor of my client. The doctor's death still didn't sit well with me. He had promised to tell me something about Buckingham. And now I would never know. I wondered if the doctor was putting me on. I wondered if he said what he said because he hated his neighbor. After all, Buckingham had called him a miserable bloke. The more I thought about it, the more I believed Dr. Carreras. I believed he had something to tell me—something I would find out later. The hard way.

No use fretting. I had a dog to find. I checked the "Lost & Found" section:

> ### LOST
> "Kula" golden retriever, male, 3 years, blond coat, at Kailua Beach Park on Sunday 6/19. $1,000 reward.

The ad ended with my office phone number. The reward, suggested by Maile and approved by Buckingham, was more than the typical stolen dog could bring on the black market.

As for "Found" pets in the classifieds, there was only one:

> ### FOUND
> Small brown female dog w/short hair and red collar in Pearl City area on 6/14.

Wrong color. Wrong size. Wrong sex. Wrong place.

The sky in the east began to glow. The beach sprang to life with early-morning walkers. Some were solitary, some in pairs, and some accompanied by canine companions that ambled alongside them or dashed into the surf after sticks and balls and floating toys. One dog looked like a spaniel, one like a black lab, another had the spots of a Dalmatian. One was a golden retriever—dark red. But no sign of Kula.

I glanced back at the *Star-Advertiser.* In the Hawai'i section, a headline and photo caught my eye:

Where Is Cheyenne Sin?
Radio Pitchman's Wife Still Missing

Cheyenne Sin had been a fashion model in her youth and still looked the part: tall and impossibly thin. Jet black hair. Skin luminescent as moonlight. In her long, shapely legs and delicate features I could see a resemblance to Lehua.

I usually have a hunch about missing-person cases. But this one wasn't sending me any strong signals. I wasn't ready to believe Mrs. Gum's theory that Buckingham murdered his wife. Nor was I ready to let him off the hook. He was a man accustomed to getting his way. But was he capable of killing anyone who might block it? Even his own wife?

To what extent Buckingham may have been involved, I could only guess. And how much the unfavorable publicity had shaken his investors' faith, I could also only guess. But I was concerned. If Buckingham went under, as the late Dr. Carreras predicted, who would pay me when my retainer ran out?

As the sun peeked above the horizon, foot traffic on the beach came to a halt. Everybody faced east like pilgrims observing a religious rite. I set down my coffee cup on the transmission hump and watched. Quite the scene. The human file glowed in the sun. Nobody moved—except the dogs. After a while I grabbed Kula's photo and walked down to get a closer look.

Before I reached the shore, the sun cleared the ocean and the rite was over. Everybody was moving again. I hailed a slim brunette in a bikini before her boxer dragged her down the beach.

"Hoku!" she commanded. "Heel!"

The boxer kept pulling.

I stepped up and flashed Kula's photo. "Have you seen this dog?"

"Looks familiar." She planted her feet in the sand as Hoku tugged at the reins. "Very familiar."

"Do you remember where you saw him last?" I was hopeful.

"Isn't he that surfing dog, the one that rides waves with the girl?"

"That's him. Have you seen him?"

"On TV."

"Right." I tried to jog her memory. "But have you seen him here on this beach?"

"Here? On Kailua Beach?"

I nodded.

"Never."

I shrugged. "Well. Thanks. If you do . . ." But Hoku had already started hauling his mistress away.

Next I tried a sandy-haired man walking a grey dog that had the gait of a racehorse.

"What kind is this?" I said to start the conversation.

"Weimaraner," he replied. "Silver, sit!" he commanded and the big dog snapped down.

"Beautiful." I handed him Kula's photo. "Ever seen this one?"

He studied Kula's image. "I saw a dog like this with a surfer on Sunday out by Flat Island."

I perked up. "What exactly did you see?"

"The golden retriever was hunched on the front of the guy's board. I saw 'em ride two or three waves. The dog never fell off. Not once. It was amazing. He just hunkered down and hung on, even in the white water."

"Could the surfer have been a girl?"

"I don't know . . . It's a long way out there." He thought for a moment. "I suppose."

"Did you see them later on the beach—either the surfer or the dog?"

"No. They were still in water when I took Silver home."

"Here's my card." I handed it to him, feeling like I'd made progress. "Please call me if you think of anything else. The golden retriever is missing. There's a reward. His owner would be very grateful for his safe return."

"OK." He took the card and Silver led him away.

Scanning the beach for my next prospect, I settled on a *tutu,* or grandmotherly type, trailing behind a fawn-colored dog that looked like a miniature hippopotamus. It had deeply wrinkled skin, a pug nose, and curling tail.

"Unusual dog," I said. "What kind is it?"

"Shar-Pei," the *tutu* said. "It's a Chinese breed."

"Are they nice dogs?"

"The best." She flashed a smile.

I handed her Kula's photo. "Ever seen this one?"

"Maybe," she said.

"Here—on Kailua Beach?" I asked.

"Not on the beach," she said, "in a car heading toward the Pali. It was on Sunday morning. Ah, two people were in the car—yeah, a man and a woman." She nodded with certainty. "The dog was in back."

"You sure it was this dog?"

"How could I miss him?" she said. "They were stopped at a red light. I stared at his pretty coat until they got the green."

"What about the two people? Was the woman a teenager with red hair?"

"No. She had black hair, I think. Definitely not red. The man was wearing a baseball cap."

"What kind of car?"

"Oh, I don't know. It was big—one of those, ah . . . SUVs. Tan or bronze." She thought for a moment. "I take it the dog shouldn't have been along for the ride?"

I nodded and handed her my card. "Please call me if you remember anything else."

"I promise," she said. Her Shar-Pei pulled her down the beach.

eleven

At eight a.m. I opened Island Insta-Print in Kailua town with my order for five hundred posters of the missing retriever. Each one listed his description and details about his disappearance—plus the $1,000 reward. The theory was that if Kula was stolen the thief might be lured by the easy money of the reward, rather than face the potential risks of reselling the dog. Even if Kula had simply wandered off, the posters would be a strong incentive to contact me.

Waiting for my order, I walked two blocks to Windward Pets and asked for the store manager, the same woman who was quoted in a story Maile had clipped. Charlene Nogata had straight black hair, brown eyes, and her ear to local gossip.

"Did you hear about that Kailua couple arrested for pet theft?" she asked.

"No," I said, "tell me."

"Spyder Silva and Reiko Infante. They're awaiting trial. The indictment says they're part of an organized pet theft ring,"

"You know them?"

"I don't know them," she said, "but I know where they live. Their address was in the paper—a front-page story a few weeks ago."

I vaguely remembered the story.

"Windward Sands apartments—about three blocks that way . . ." She pointed in the direction I had come. "Behind Aloha Auto Parts."

"Eh, thanks. I have time to kill."

"They're not the kind of people you'd want to meet in a back alley," she said.

"Understood."

"Sleazy." She pointed again towards the Windward Sands.

* * *

I hiked a few blocks and there it was. In the long shadow cast by the auto parts store stood a faded brown apartment building. It had seen better days: cracked and missing jalousies, rotting wood trim, and a parking lot that looked more like a wrecking yard. Not the sort of place you'd normally find a pedigree dog. Among a row of mailboxes on the ground floor, I found the names Silva & Infante. Apartment 1J.

It was a corner unit and I had to knock three times before someone answered. When the door finally opened there stood a man, naked from the waist up. Tattoos covered every inch of skin I could see. The largest one, on his chest, showed crossed assault rifles coiled with a cobra. Beneath that was: KILL 'EM ALL, LET GOD SORT 'EM OUT.

Sleazy. I could see what the pet store owner meant. Though I wasn't shaking in my boots. Guys like him were mostly show.

"Watchu want?" He reeked of sardines.

"Are you Spyder Silva?"

He nodded.

Behind him, a hard looking woman lounged on a sofa having a smoke. Her stained robe suggested she had just rolled out of bed. Reiko Infante?

I handed him my card, showed him Kula's photo, and hauled out my pidgin. "Evah see dis dog?"

"Who wen' send you heah?" Silva snarled.

"One neighbor ovah dere." I pointed vaguely in the direction of Windward Pets.

"Dey wrong, brah. I nevah seen dis dog." He started to close the door.

I stepped forward. "What kine car you drive?"

"Spyder!" the woman shouted. "Tell 'em to fuck off."

"Shut up, awready." The man handed me back my card. "Da black Toyota truck in da lot. Go check 'em out." The door slammed in my face.

I wandered back out to the parking lot and before long found the black pickup. It was raised high with knobby off-road tires and displayed a bumper sticker: *P.E.T.A.—People Eating Tasty Animals.* But it wasn't bronze. Or an SUV. I peeked inside. Unbelievable. On the floor in front of the passenger seat was an automatic pistol. It looked like a Beretta. Silva ought to think twice about leaving his weapon in plain view, especially when he and his playmate were under indictment. But he didn't strike me as the thinking type.

I walked away shaking my head. Though the tips I'd been getting so far added up to nothing, the two alleged pet thieves had scored a spot on my suspect list. Despite the fact that Kula didn't appear to be inside their apartment and that Silva's truck looked nothing like a tan SUV, it was too much of a coincidence that he and Infante were awaiting trial for pet theft. And that they lived in Kailua, less than a mile from where Kula disappeared. Plus, I flat out didn't like either one of them.

* * *

Five hundred posters in hand, I made my way among the businesses of Kailua town, asking if shop owners would display them. Most were cooperative. And many offered heartfelt stories about the time their own Mele or Kaipo or Duke went missing.

My cell phone beeped. Madison Highcamp. She left a text message:

Tonight.

I didn't reply. I knew what she meant.

Then I drove to Lanikai Elementary School, on the edge of Kailua Beach. The Principal's husband, Creighton Lee, ran HPD's photo lab and was a surfing buddy. I'd never met his wife, Marianne. She looked to be in her mid-forties. She was pretty and slightly plump.

"Kai," she smiled warmly. "It's so nice to meet you. Creighton's told me so much about you."

I cringed.

"He calls you a 'soul surfer.' And to Creighton that's good."

Soul surfer meant someone who surfs for the love of riding waves—not for competition, not for glory, not to be cool, not for any other reason than pure passion.

"Creighton's too generous," I said. "He's the original soul surfer. I can't compare with him."

"So," she looked at me curiously, "what brings you to Lanikai Elementary?"

"A famous surfing dog. Maybe you've heard of him? His name is Kula."

She looked puzzled. "No, afraid I— "

Then I pleaded my case. I had a missing dog to find, time was of the essence, and her students could help by putting up posters. Not only that, I would pay.

She told me to wait outside the fifth and sixth grade rooms while, just before recess, she repeated my spiel. As the kids trotted out, three volunteered. Noe and Tiffy, two giggly girls who looked like twins, and Ronson, a cool dude in a North Shore t-shirt. The three of them were friends. After I called their parents for approval, we agreed to meet at the end of the school day.

In the meantime, I returned to my Kailua Beach stakeout. Dog-walkers were few and far between that time of day, I found out, and the dog-less folks I approached offered no help.

When school let out I picked up my student helpers. I put my surfboard on the roof racks to make room inside the Impala. They were enthusiastic. I found out each one had a pet. Ronson's family had a bichon frise, Noe's a black Lab, and Tiffy's a wayward parakeet named Blu. The two girls, it turned out, were not twins. They just looked alike. The kids chatted about their pets while I drove from one utility pole to the next. The girls' giggles went away once we got down to business. I mentioned the likelihood that Kula was stolen.

"Why would anybody steal a dog?" Noe asked.

I could have given her a list of reasons, but I just shrugged. The reasons wouldn't have answered her question anyway, which was more like, "What would possess a person to do something like that?" For that question I really had no answer.

Soon I was giving the kids directions. "Tiffy, you take the posters." I handed her about a dozen. "Noe, here's the staple gun." I gave her the heavy chrome gun.

"What do I do?" Ronson asked.

"The most important job. You watch for traffic while they put up the posters." Then I reassured him. "Don't worry. You're going to take turns with the jobs."

At each pole Tiffy popped out with a poster and Noe with the staple gun. Ronson guarded by watching and directing traffic. After a dozen poles, as promised, the kids changed roles. Between stops they entertained me with stories of pet misadventures—like the time Tiffy had to climb a mango tree to get her parakeet.

By the end of three hours, we'd covered the entire Lanikai loop, all side streets dog-walkers would use to get to the beach, and also parts of Kailua town near the water. My helpers got home before dinner and walked away with fifteen dollars each, all promising to keep an eye out for Kula.

After I dropped off the last of the three, Noe's question was still ringing in my ears: Why would anybody steal a dog?

twelve

Back at Kailua Beach Park, I removed my board from the racks, slipped off my khakis from over my board shorts, and paddled out to Flat Island. My plan was to unwind and work the case at the same time. Regulars out there might know something about Kula. And by waiting for the after-work crowd I hoped to catch some of the same surfers who were likely to be there weekends—the time that the golden retriever had disappeared.

My young helpers' happy stories about their pets got me thinking about when I had a dog. Pono was a shepherd-golden mix, a light-colored *poi* dog that looked a little like Kula. Except Pono's ears kind of half stood up like a shepherd's and half flopped over like a retriever's, in a homely, adorable way. He and I were inseparable. Until I lost him.

As I stroked toward the coral island a quarter mile off shore, its unusual shape came into view. A few acres long, the oblong island resembled a green tabletop, barely above the high tide mark. It was a bird sanctuary where you can watch pairs of seabirds nesting in *pukas,* or holes, in the coral. But most people come for the surf, rather than for the birds. On a good day, waves sweep around the south side of the island like a point break. You ride the wave to your left, steering clear of the rocks and coral heads in the shallow water near the island.

The trade winds gently drifted by as I paddled out. The water in the lee of the island was like glass and I could see the rocky bottom clearly. A half dozen surfers were having fun with a three-foot swell. I paddled into the lineup and caught a wave, riding left with my back to the curl, like any "regular foot" does. Then I paddled back and waited for another. I sat on my board, dangling my toes in the water. *Lucky you live Hawai'i,* as the saying goes.

One surf buddy of mine calls Flat Island a shark pit. But I've never seen a shark here. And I haven't heard of anyone getting bitten. But I found myself scouring the ocean for a dark shape. The semi-circle of welts on my chest always reminded me of the time I got hit at Laniākea.

It happened so fast I didn't see it coming. A tiger shark. Fortunately he didn't like the taste of me. He took one bite and swam off. There was lots of blood in the water, but nothing broken except my skin. I paddled in under my own power, with an escort of surfers who couldn't believe their eyes. The EMS guys gave me a ride to Kahuku Hospital. I got lucky. I didn't even stay overnight. But ever since then whenever I go surfing I say a mantra, "No Fear, No Fear," and I try to forget.

Of the dozen or so surfers at Flat Island that afternoon, I found only one who'd actually been in the water on Sunday when Kula disappeared. A deeply-tanned Rastafarian dude named Dickie. But the dreadlocked surfer could tell me nothing new.

Dickie and I sat in the lineup together and eventually I caught a wave with him, giving him the sweetest part of the curl. After that ride he pointed toward shore, waved, and started paddling in. As he was stroking away, he cocked his head back and said, "You betta go talk wit' Moku."

"What's his numbah?"

"Doan know, brah."

I shouted mine to him across the water. "Tell Moku for call me, yeah?"

"Latahs." Dickie was soon out of earshot.

When I paddled in later, a yellow helicopter buzzed me on its way to Flat Island. On its belly was FIRE AND RESCUE. It circled the island and then hovered over the lineup, whipping whitecaps where surfers were sitting on their boards. I wondered what was up.

Once on shore I spotted two HPD cruisers, blue lights flashing. Down in the swimming area at Kailua Beach Park, no one was in the water. Guys in trunks and girls in bikinis were standing on shore, staring out to sea. Another surfer who had been at Flat Island said, "Did you see the shark?"

"What shark?"

"Tiger. Ten foot. Swimming toward Flat Island."

Shark Pit. Had my buddy been right?

I looked on the beach for Dickie. He was gone. I doubted I would ever hear from him or his friend Moku. Shouting my phone number across the water had been a long shot.

But so far, long shots were all I had.

thirteen

On the way back from Kailua, I swung by Maile's cottage to feed her cats. It should have been easy.

Peppah, the dusty black Angora, pounced on me the minute I walked in the door, meowing and clawing his way up my leg. Coconut, the Siamese, stretched casually on the sofa. The calico, Lolo, gave me one look and ripped into a bedroom.

After I fixed their food and set out three dishes—each inscribed with a name in calligraphy—Peppah and Coconut came running, but not Lolo. I went looking. I ended up in Maile's bedroom, her parents' bedroom when we were kids, finally spotting Lolo under the poster bed. *"Auwē!"* I said under my breath—the pidgin equivalent of dammit.

Once I left Maile's cottage, Peppah or Coconut or both would devour Lolo's dinner. The shy cat would go hungry. I couldn't have that on my conscience. So down on my knees I went, wondering how I'd got this gig.

"Come out, Lolo," I urged her. "Come out girl."

She retreated farther. I checked my watch. I had a dinner date at six.

Only one solution: I slipped her food dish under the bed. It went in easily for about a foot, then it hit something. I leaned down and saw an object—flat and slightly smaller than a shoebox lid. I moved it to the side and inched Lolo's food dish toward her.

When I leaned back on my heels, the object caught the light. I pulled it out. It was a picture frame holding a photo of Maile and her late husband Nestor standing arm-in-arm at the Koko Head firing range. The day was sunny and Nestor had his shirt off. He was a well-built man, his body and arms packed with muscle. Maile was all smiles. Between them was propped the same sniper rifle from the photo in her living room. *A day on the range.*

Seeing the two of them so happy together gave me a sinking feeling. First Karl, then Nester. Why did it still bother me that I wanted Maile once and couldn't have her? High school was years ago. Was I feeling something for Maile again? I nudged the photo back beneath the bed, curious why she kept it there. But not before looking at it one more time.

It must have been tough for Maile when Nestor died. And tough again when Rusty disappeared. It was all too familiar. I had Pono when my parents died. My Auntie Mae Kealoha told me that my mother and father had gone to heaven and that I mustn't worry about them because they were in a wonderful place, more wonderful than I could ever imagine. My father's rented airplane had crashed into cloud-shrouded Mauna Kea on the Big Island, the tallest mountain in the Pacific. Auntie Mae explained that I would never see him or my mother again in this life, but if I was a good boy and lived a good life I would see them in the next. My father, mother, and I would all live happily together for eternity.

That sounded good to my eight-year-old ears. But the eternal happiness didn't seem quite complete, so I asked, "What about Pono? Will he live with us in Heaven, too?"

She hardly skipped a beat. "Is Pono a good dog?"

"He's a very good dog," I said proudly.

Auntie tried to smile through her tears. "Yes, Pono will live with you forever."

I was relieved. Until I grew older and realized how long I'd have to wait for that promised bliss.

Under the poster bed, Lolo finally started to nibble on her dinner. Safe for me to go.

* * *

I drove from Maile's cottage to my studio apartment at the Waikīkī Edgewater to shower off from my session at Flat Island. "Edgewater" is kind of a stretch, since the building sits nearly half a mile from the beach. But the Edgewater does in fact flank the Ala Wai Canal. My own tiny flat on the forty-fifth floor is wedged between two penthouses and faces the airport and Pearl Harbor. It's the less glamorous view compared to the view of Diamond Head, in the opposite direction. But on a clear day I can pick out Ford Island, the Arizona Memorial, and the Mighty Mo. And beyond them, the majestic Waianae Range.

I hopped into my tiny shower, about the size of a coffin standing on its head. My bathroom and the entire apartment, for that matter, are not much bigger than a walk-in closet and resemble a discount Waikīkī hotel room, with bath and kitchenette at one end, and *lānai*, or patio, at the other. Against one wall are a double bed and nightstand with the photo of a former girlfriend. Against the other, a color TV on top of a dresser.

Above that hangs a photo of my mom and dad. Next to them a surf poster. And that's it.

Before leaving for dinner I checked my messages. I was surprised to find one from Maile. She had arrived in Salt Lake City and driven to the pet refuge. She was looking forward to the four-day workshop on animal sanctuaries that began the next morning. She thanked me again for giving her a ride to the airport and feeding her cats. She even thanked me in advance for meeting her plane on Saturday.

"I'm looking forward to catching up with you, Kai . . ." She paused. "It's been too long."

It had.

Then she said, "If it turns out Kula didn't just wander off, if it turns out he was stolen, watch yourself. Pet thieves are a twisted lot. A dog is just a pawn to them. They're usually after something else—to gain advantage over someone or something. I've run into cases like that, where the dog's master owes money or has a vindictive ex. It has nothing to do with the animal and everything to do with the people. Good luck, Kai. And watch yourself."

fourteen

I had dinner that night at the posh Waikīkī Canoe Club with Madison Highcamp—Mrs. Conrad Highcamp—third wife of a wealthy hotelier whose luxury resorts dotted the globe.

Madison commanded a prime oceanfront table on the open-air *lānai*. She was puffing on a cigarette, sipping a martini, and talking nonstop on her cell phone when I arrived. Her Maltese, balled into a white puff, leaped from her lap and danced around me, yipping and making a spectacle of herself.

"Twinkie, hush!" Madison set down her phone and stood. Her dark cherry hair, pinned up in loose curls, almost tumbled down onto a beach cover-up that covered very little at all. But nobody was complaining. The former beauty queen wasn't shy about showing herself off. She mashed out her cigarette, picked up the dog, and pressed her glossy red lips on my cheek.

"Hello, darling." She smelled of Chanel, tobacco, and gin. It was a provocative, come-hither blend of odors like ripe cheddar in a mousetrap. Madison Highcamp spent her days shopping designer boutiques and sunning on the beach, and her nights hanging out in private clubs and dancing at charity balls. Her Midas-touch husband was old enough to be her father, or grandfather. She lived in a sprawling Diamond Head penthouse, while he preferred their Beverly Hills mansion, closer to his corporate headquarters in Los Angeles. They were seldom together.

I met Madison through a Canoe Club paddler who urged me to call her, saying she was lonely and enjoyed the company of surfers. "I don't date married women," I said. He persisted: "Spread some *aloha,* Kai." Against my better judgment I called her.

"Let's have a drink." She sat and planted a kiss on the Maltese's wet noise. *"Twinkie, precious!"* she whispered in the dog's ear.

"You should get a pet, Kai. You're alone too much. A nice dog like Twinkie might do wonders."

"First Tommy. Now you."

"What?" she asked.

"Never mind." The cocktail waitress came so I said: "What would you like to drink?"

"The same." She pointed to her empty martini glass.

"A martini for the lady," I told the waitress. "And a beer for me."

As the sun sunk toward the Pacific in a riot of gold, Madison waxed eloquent. "Ah, the islands," she said. "Is there anything like them?"

"Lucky you live Hawai'i," I said.

"Conrad hates it here," she said. "Can you believe that?"

"How can anyone hate Hawai'i?"

"Oh, I think he finds the islands lovely and all. But there's nothing here for him. No captains of industry on the scale he's used to. No tycoons or politicians of his stripe. No glamour of Hollywood. He prefers Beverly Hills and Palm Springs and sometimes New York."

"So he doesn't ever visit you?"

"The chances of him coming are about the same as snow falling in Waikīkī. Anyway, he knows I have friends. He's not stupid."

Our drinks came.

"Cheers," I said.

Madison's midnight eyes met mine. I studied her perfect teeth and marveled at how different we were. The fortyish perfumed debutante who never worked a day in her life and the thirty-four year old surfer and P.I. who was perpetually broke. We had almost nothing in common. But in a strange way, we did. We were both adrift on this lonely planet, as Tommy called it. Why should I question our arrangement? Maybe it was Tommy's question that was bothering me: Are you still hanging out with that Highcamp woman? He had hit a nerve. Or maybe it was seeing Maile again after all those years.

"Kai." Madison rested her chin on jeweled fingers. "Let's not go so long between rendezvous. You know how I miss you."

"I miss you too," I heard myself saying.

Her cell phone rang.

"Hello," she said cheerfully. Her expression suddenly changed. "Conrad?" She put her hand over the mouthpiece and whispered to me, *"Oh my god!"* Then she removed her hand. "Surprised to hear from you, darling . . . I'm at the Canoe Club having dinner with a friend." She reached across the table and took my hand.

"Oh, nobody you know." Madison winked at me. "Drinking . . . ? Just my usual martini before dinner." She reached for another cigarette, then frowned. "You're coming to Hawai'i?" The cigarette rested between her fingers. "Oh, anytime you like, darling. It's up to you . . . OK, love you too."

Madison's glossy lips tightened as she snapped her phone shut. I leaned forward with a lit match. "Conrad is threatening to come here again," she said. "Probably to check up on me." The flame caught the tip of her cigarette as she puffed and made it glow. "He always says he's coming, but he never does."

"Never?" I shook the match out.

"Almost never." She shrugged. "Let's eat, honey, and not talk about Conrad.

We called the waitress and ordered dinner—a warm cilantro and marinated quail salad for Madison and Canoe Club burger for me.

"Why don't you tell me all about one of your exciting cases?" Madison's eyes glittered.

"OK." I fingered the condensation dripping down my beer glass. How could I admit I'd been reduced to searching for a dog? Then I thought of Twinkie, sleeping peacefully in Madison's lap. A dog lover, maybe she would sympathize? I gave her an abridged version of the story, hinting at, but not naming my client. She figured it out. It's a small island.

"Barry Buckingham, the gold dealer?" she asked.

"You know him?"

"Slightly," she said evasively.

"How'd you meet?"

"Conrad, bless his heart, gave me a little investment money to play with—barely six figures—and I thought, why not buy some gold? After all, I love gold." She waved her rings at me. "Anyway, the other day I was driving home from Neiman's and heard him on the radio: *'I'm certified gold expert Barry Buckingham, and you're listening to Gold Standard.'* He has such a soothing voice, you know. So British."

"Australian, I believe."

"Why he just captivated me," Madison continued, as if I hadn't spoken. "So I called him at his 'offices,' as he says on the radio, and we chatted. His voice was even more soothing than on the air. And then," she took a sip of her martini, "he invited me to dinner on his yacht tomorrow night. Can you believe that?"

I could. "Be careful," I cautioned.

"Don't worry, I'm just going to listen to what he has to say." She played with a loose curl. "Have you ever thought of investing, Kai? A nest egg for your future?"

"No." Madison had no idea how the other half lived.

"Maybe you should consider gold. Barry says it's very stable."

The waitress arrived with Madison's salad and my burger. Madison stubbed out her cigarette. We had barely taken a bite when her phone rang again.

"Hello." She made a puzzled look. *"Barry . . . ?* Oh, of course. Yes, I'm looking forward. Seven? That would be fine. See you then." She closed her phone.

"Let me guess what Barry Buckingham wanted to talk about."

"Gold . . ." she said.

Madison Highcamp—rich, idle, and beautiful—would be a prime target for smooth talkers with something glittery to sell.

"And to reconfirm dinner," she continued. "I guess he's at loose ends."

"Did you know his wife disappeared—Cheyenne Sin?"

"That was *his* wife? I didn't put two and two together."

"Four months ago," I said. "I thought Buckingham was hiring me to find her. Instead I'm looking for his dog."

"Poor man."

"Me or him?"

"Both of you."

"It's a gig." I didn't bother to tell her that HPD, and one of his neighbors, suspected Buckingham in his wife's disappearance. Madison would meet him and make up her own mind.

She fixed those eyes on me again. "Why don't you come back to my penthouse after dinner, and we can . . . talk."

"I have to get up early, Madison . . ."

She leaned forward, her breasts brushing the white linen tablecloth. "You know I'm not good with *no*'s."

"Just for a little while," I finally agreed.

"Good. You can show me your shark bite."

We both knew what that meant.

* * *

After we finished dinner, billed, against my polite objections to Conrad Highcamp's account, I walked Madison to her Diamond Head apartment, a few minutes' stroll from the Canoe Club. Her penthouse was one of only two on the entire top floor and commanded a sweeping view of Waikīkī. The view was dark at night, except for the lights of the beachfront hotels reflecting in the surf. We sat on a couch and Madison drank another martini. About half way down she got to thinking. A dangerous thing.

"Why can't I be more like you, Kai, and surf all day in the sun?"

"What's stopping you?" I said. "You've got more time and money than anybody I know." I could have told her I hadn't surfed all day since I opened my detective agency, but she wouldn't have heard me.

"Let me see your shark bite."

"Why do you want to see it again? You'll make yourself afraid of the ocean and then you'll never surf."

"I don't know," she said. "It's just so . . . wild."

"Wild? I never thought of it that way."

She pouted.

"OK. Here." I pulled up my shirt.

Madison's eyes widened and then she explored the sixteen welts with her fingertips. "You think I have everything, Kai, but you're wrong."

"You can have whatever you want."

"No I can't," she sobbed. "I'm not free." She pulled me down with her on the couch.

I don't remember much after that. Those nights we spent together in her apartment tended to blur. I've had finer moments. Madison and I both knew what we had couldn't last, but tomorrow didn't matter as long as we had tonight.

It was nearly one when I left her apartment. Wheeling my Impala through the drowsy streets of Waikīkī, I felt more alone than when the night began. And I was no closer to finding the elusive retriever. But I had learned about the gold dealer's tactics with the rich and gorgeous.

fifteen

Thursday morning's *Star-Advertiser* carried a brief story in the Hawai'i News section about Dr. Carreras. The police investigation had determined that his accident was caused by a combination of the rain-slick surface of upper Tantalus Drive and the excessive speed of the Porsche. Alcohol was not a factor.

I wondered again what Dr. Carreras was going to tell me about Buckingham.

Later that morning I pulled into my parking stall off Maunakea Street and walked to my office at the corner of Beretania above Fujiyama's Flower Leis. Parking in that part of Chinatown was murderously expensive. Thankfully Mrs. Fujiyama had three stalls reserved for her tenants. She could probably rent them for almost as much as her offices.

As I walked to the lei shop, the case started stirring up memories again of my dog, Pono.

* * *

When my parents died it was a comfort to have Pono. The Kealoha family *hānaied* me and I moved from town to their

Punaluʻu home, across from the beach on Oʻahu's windward side. Pono came too. I attended school at Kahuku and had trouble adjusting. My grades tumbled. It was soon decided that I would move again, this time to the mainland to live with my Uncle Orson's family in Pasadena, California, and go to school there. My Auntie promised to take care of Pono until I got settled, then ship him to me.

After I'd been in California a few weeks, my uncle got a call from Oʻahu. He sat me down at the kitchen table, a somber expression on his face. "I have some bad news for you, Kai. Your dog was run over by a car. He didn't survive."

Pono's death, coming on the heels of my parents' accident—and without my Auntie's promises of heavenly bliss—was almost too much to bear. Later she sent me Pono's collar and license. I think I still have them somewhere in my apartment, along with her note promising I would see my dog again in Heaven with my parents. After that I couldn't imagine having another dog. And I never did. I never even gave dogs much thought—until this case.

* * *

Inside the flower shop Mrs. Fujiyama and two of her *lei* girls, Chastity and Joon, were stringing tuberose. The powerful scent raised the hair on my neck and followed me up the orange shag stairs. At the end of the hall, I stopped in front of the full-color longboard rider airbrushed on my door. Beneath were the words: Surfing Detective: Confidential Investigations—All Islands. Under those words I felt like scrawling: *No missing pet cases.* But it was too late.

Inside my office the red light on the answering machine was blinking. I hadn't checked for messages since yesterday. There were seven.

The first: "Can you help us find Puffy? She's a Persian cat. She wandered off two days ago. She usually comes right back. But we've looked everywhere. We live in 'Ālewa Heights . . ."

The second: "Max is missing and I don't know what to do. He's an Airedale and he's my only companion since my husband died. Maybe you are my godsend. Please, please call me . . ."

The third: "Is this the pet detective? I found a dog . . . Uh, a black dog in Palolo . . . and I wondered if you could help me find its owner."

The fourth: "Hello, this is Mrs. Leong. I have a favor to ask. Could you help me pick a pedigree Skye Terrier puppy for my granddaughter?"

Who was referring these people? 'Ālewa Heights? Palolo? They were nowhere near my posters in Kailua. Maybe it was my ads in the two daily papers? But no mention had been made of a pet detective. Go figure.

The fifth call came from a man who remembered seeing a leather collar embossed in gold on Kailua Beach. But he went on to say: "I came back the next day and the collar was gone." I filed that one away in my mental notebook.

The sixth call: "You want fine' one golden retrievah? Try one puppy mill in Mililani. She got all kine." He left an address that I copied down.

The last call: "I found your dog." The voice sounded old, male, Caucasian. "He's a light-colored retriever with no collar. My wife and I live near Kailua Beach. He wandered here yesterday, but I just saw your poster this morning on our walk."

The man left a number and said he didn't want the reward, just for the "beautiful retriever" to be returned to his family.

I called immediately. Maybe I'd gotten lucky.

An old woman said her husband wasn't home, but that I could come claim the sunny retriever, as she described him.

"Is the dog male?" I asked.

"Yes," she replied. "He's male, and he's very pretty."

"Sounds like Kula." I was hopeful.

She gave me her address off south Kalaheo, less than two blocks from Kailua Beach Park where Kula had disappeared.

* * *

My Impala was purring over the Pali again, windward bound. The address the woman had given me was on a quiet beachside street in the residential tract of Kuʻulei. I pulled up to a ranch-style home that looked comfortably middle class. The sound of my door slamming set off a deep, authoritative barking from behind a palm hedge. The bark obviously came from a big dog.

I walked around to the front door and rang the bell. A gray-haired woman wearing a flowered *muʻumuʻu* that hung on her like a sack invited me in. As she led me to her backyard, she rambled on about the found dog.

"He's a beauty. So shiny. And his eyes . . . but you know that." She opened her screen door. "My husband doesn't care about the reward. He just wants to give the dog back to its owner."

"That's generous," I said, "but the reward is his, so long as the dog is Kula."

"It's him all right," she said. "Follow me."

We stepped onto a huge lawn so perfect it looked like a putting green. Encircling it were birds-of-paradise, red ginger, and *laua'e* ferns. I spotted the dog wandering among the plants, sniffing then lifting his leg. The moment he heard us he charged in our direction, tail wagging, almost knocking me over. This was a big, gregarious dog and his enthusiasm was over the top.

"Calm down, boy." I patted his yellow head. It wasn't Kula. "I think this is a Labrador," I said, "a yellow Labrador. He's got a shorter coat than a golden and looks a bit stockier."

"Oh," the woman said, her disappointment obvious.

"Have you called the Humane Society?" I asked.

"No. When my husband saw your poster we decided to call you first."

"Well, somebody is probably worried sick about this dog."

She nodded. "He's a beauty, all right."

I thanked her for calling me, left a poster with Kula's photo, and drove away. I don't know who was more disappointed, the old woman or me.

sixteen

I hopped onto the H-3 freeway, climbed into the Koʻolau mountains, shot through the tunnel, and headed for the leeward side. My destination was Mililani Town, where my anonymous caller had said I might find a puppy mill. Another questionable lead. But it was worth a try.

As I drove, I reviewed Buckingham's three possible suspects—two neighbors and an alleged prowler. Neither of the neighbors got me any closer to the missing dog and neither promised to be any help. Mrs. Gum's grip on reality seemed iffy, at best, and Dr. Carreras was dead. And I had found no evidence of any prowler to back Buckingham's allegation. Mostly what I had come away with were allegations against Buckingham himself—that he was a con man, fraud, potential bankrupt, and murderer.

My own fledgling efforts at pet detection had uncovered two indicted pet thieves, Spyder Silva and Reiko Infante, but neither as yet could be linked to Kula's disappearance. My dawn stakeout of Kailua beach yielded a possible sighting of Kula in an SUV leaving town, but so far I couldn't corroborate it. A surf session at Flat Island turned up a possible informant named Moku, who I had no way to contact. And he hadn't bothered to call me. My newspaper ads and posters were eliciting calls, mostly from desperate pet owners looking for their own lost Fido or Fluffy. Finally, my one promising lead to a light-colored retriever evaporated when the dog turned out to be a yellow Lab.

So here I was driving into central Oʻahu on the H-2, hoping for a breakthrough. I exited at Mililani Town, where pineapple and cane fields in the plateau between the Waiʻanae and Koʻolau ranges had been transformed into a crowded suburb of condos, townhouses, and tract homes. And also puppy mills?

The main goal of a puppy mill, Maile had told me, is to make money. Its owners don't give a rip about the health and living conditions of the puppies, or about the moms and pops that produce them. I wasn't looking forward to my visit. Criminals I run into on my everyday cases make me feel bad enough about human beings. I didn't relish the thought of meeting up with lowlifes who abuse helpless animals to fatten their wallets.

I drove along Meheula Parkway past a couple of schools, a park, and a recreation center, scouting for one particular townhouse among a sea of thousands. The address I was given by the anonymous caller was not on a street, it turned out, but a court in a secluded tract abutting the park.

The cream and baby blue townhouse had a carport with an empty mailbox—I checked—attached to one of its pillars. A grimy Jeep Cherokee wearing a Schofield Barracks sticker was parked under a portico with purple hydrangea and parched palms. A faded and torn American flag hung over the doorway.

As I approached the front door, a rotten smell crept up on me like a dead skunk. Then I heard an animal whimpering. I take that back. Not one animal—many.

I rang the bell and heard shuffling feet.

"Yeah, whadda ya want?" a woman's voice boomed through the door.

"A golden retriever," I shouted back.

The door creaked open to a fortyish dirty blonde sinking her teeth into a strawberry danish. She didn't need the danish. She had a double chin, ballooning breasts, and a sagging belly that strained her oversized T-shirt.

"How'd ya fine my place?" she asked with a full mouth. "My newspaper ads don' give no address."

"I asked around."

She swallowed her danish and let me in. Her townhouse looked fairly typical. Pale green walls, one bedroom downstairs and probably two more upstairs. A couple of baths. And a narrow kitchen with an electric range, microwave and fridge. What wasn't typical was the smell. And the mess. The place was a garbage heap. A six-pack of diet cola was perched on a rusty exercise bicycle; a case of rum sat in a laundry basket—four quarts left. The others empty. But I saw no dogs.

"What's your name?" She glanced at me with sad blue eyes.

"Tommy." I borrowed my attorney's name. "And you are?" I asked.

"Lou," she grunted. "So you' look'n for a golden retriever puppy?"

I nodded.

"Jus' a minute, Tommy." She put her plump hands on her hips. "My pups aren't ready yet, but you can look 'em over and pick one in advance."

Lou led me into a tiny half bath where a dull red bitch was nursing a half dozen scrawny pups on a bare tile floor. No bed. No blanket. The dog's tummy was so sunken I could have encircled it with my hands. And I could count her ribs. Every one stood out like a rack of lamb. Her puppies were drinking her dry.

"Check 'em out, Tommy." Lou hovered over me as I knelt down. The odor coming off the pups made my eyes water. My stomach turned, partly from the stench, partly from what I saw.

"Seventy-five dollars cash will hold a pup. It's how I pay the rent. My husband got hurt in Iraq. He's been at Tripler Hospital for months, but he ain't never gonna be the same again. Never."

"I'm sorry," I said.

"It ain't easy," she said. "We was gonna retire together, have our own kennel, and breed champions. But then . . ."

"I like this one." I pointed to one of the pups, then realized this wasn't getting me any closer to Kula. "But I'd like to see your adult dogs, too."

"Adult dogs?" She clucked her tongue. "You said you wanted a puppy!"

"I thought I did. But now that I've seen them, I don't know. Maybe one of each."

"Follow me." She trudged across a stinky carpet to a tiny bedroom. There were four crates, each containing a dark dog. Like the one in the bathroom, these adult dogs were also severely malnourished. Rib and hip bones protruding. Stomachs concave. No sign of Kula.

"These are fine," I said, "but I'd hoped for a light-colored dog. A male."

"A blond male?" she said. "I've got just the one. He's a beauty. But it'll take me a day or two to get him."

"Where is he?" I tried not to sound too excited.

"Jus' give me a call tomorrow." She recited a phone number, and walked me to the front door. "You can decide about the puppy then."

"OK, Lou," I said, forcing a smile. "Till tomorrow."

She smiled back, red jelly still between her teeth. I left feeling almost sad for Lou. But sadder for her dogs. I wondered if I was cut out for pet detection.

I knew the answer, but thought the reason was that I didn't know the ropes. But maybe I just didn't have the heart, or the stomach, to deal with animal abusers. Then I put my feelings aside and asked myself a question more pertinent to the case: Could this particular abuser deliver the famous surfing dog?

* * *

By the time I got back to my office I had two more phone messages. The first was an urgent plea to find an African grey parrot. I deleted it. The second got my attention:

"You like get da dog back, brah? Bettah geev' me one call."

It was a male voice and his phone number had a 259 prefix—Waimānalo, a good five miles from Kailua where Kula disappeared. Was it likely that a dog could have wandered that far along the heavily-trafficked Kalaniana'ole Highway that connects the two towns? Doubtful. If Kula was in Waimānalo, he had been driven there.

I dialed the number. Once I identified myself, the same male voice from the message said, "You get da t'ousand-dollah reward, brah?"

"I get da money, if you get da dog." Well, Buckingham had the money, but I could get it.

"Bring da money if you like get da dog."

"Weah I bring it?"

"I goin' tell you weah, brah."

I heard mumbling in the background, two or three more male voices in garbled pidgin. The caller came back.

"Da end of Kapu Road in Waimānalo. Know weah dat is?"

"Dono." I played dumb.

"Wen you in da valley, head *mauka*. Pass da nurseries. Den you goin' hit one dead end. Come tonight, eleven o'clock. No try bring nobody wit' you."

"What your name, brah?" I asked.

"Moku."

"Da surfah?"

"Das me."

"OK, Moku. Bring da dog or no deal."

"I bring da dog. You bring da t'ousand.

seventeen

I called Buckingham and asked if I could see him. About to begin his daily radio program, he suggested we meet later at his yacht club for a dinner sail. I agreed to meet, but declined the sail and the dinner, saying I had to follow a lead that night that might shed light on Kula's disappearance. I also wanted to avoid running into Madison, who I knew was on the guest list.

"Good on ya, mate!" Buckingham replied in his Australian lingo. "That's the best possible regret. Tell me more."

"I'll fill you in when I see you," I said. "I'd rather not discuss it on the phone."

"No worries," he said.

"Say, too bad about your neighbor," I said, referring to Dr. Carreras. "But I gather you didn't like him much."

"Dreadful news," Buckingham said. "I didn't care for the man, but I certainly didn't want him dead." My client said this in a curious way, leaving the impression that if he'd wanted the doctor dead, he would have made it happen.

On my way to the yacht club I stopped at Maile's cottage to feed her cats. An instant replay of the night before. Peppah clawed his way up my pants leg, Coconut flaked out on the sofa, and Lolo hotfooted it into Maile's bedroom.

I brought Lolo's food to the bedroom and got down on my knees.

"Come out, girl." I looked under the bed frame. Nothing. I peered into the darkness for some sign of movement. "Lolo?"

Nothing. Then I noticed Maile's closet door was ajar. I crossed the room and pushed it open further. "Come out girl. I've got places to go."

The closet was dark and smelled of mold. If Lolo was in there, I couldn't see her. Then at the edge of the closet I noticed a long, round object leaning against the doorframe. I had no business snooping in the closet of my old friend, but being nosy is an occupational hazard. I reached in and pulled it out. Maile's rifle. The Remington was a serious tactical weapon—bolt action, carbon-fiber stock, stainless steel barrel, and a scope. On impulse, I sighted through the scope. Maile's bed looked huge in its crisp crosshairs. The precision was awesome.

I knew precision when I saw it because I'd fired more weapons than the average person. After I surfed myself out of college in my freshman year, against my Uncle Orson's advice I joined the army. He paid big bucks to send me to Flintridge Prep and to Point Loma College, so he was disappointed. But even though Point Loma had three of the best surf spots in San Diego—Garbage, Ab, and New Break—I found out fast that academic life wasn't for me. So when a recruiter dangled a cushy job back home at Fort DeRussy in Waikīkī in front of me, I bit.

It didn't happen. I was never stationed in Waikīkī. I went to Fort Ord in Monterey, which closed a few years after I left,

and trained for the infantry. Handguns, automatic rifles, gre-
nade launchers, machine guns, wire-guided missiles. You name
it, I shot it. I'm not a gun guy, and I think the world would be
a better place without them, but circumstances have forced me
to become familiar with a wide variety. Later when I became a
PI, in order to register my .357 I took a course in which I shot
Glocks, Sigs, Berretas, and Smith & Wessons—handguns used
by law enforcement and the military. This, plus my infantry
experience, is why I know more about firearms than the average person, and why I could appreciate the Remington.

I returned the weapon to Maile's closet and wondered how
long it had been since she had fired it. Then I scolded myself
for poking around in her things. She had trusted me, as an old
friend, with her cats and her cottage, and here I was violating
that trust. And getting closer to her, despite my resolve not to.

"OK, Lolo. Here's your food." I set the dish by the open
closet and turned to leave. The timid cat was going to have to
fend for herself.

* * *

The Ala Moana Yacht Club hugged the Diamond Head end
of the beach park and Ala Wai Harbor. I wandered the posh
facilities looking for Buckingham. First I tried the clubhouse
that sat smack on the harbor. My client wasn't in the waterfront
bar or the *koa*-paneled dining room or the lava rock swimming
pool. Then I headed out to the boat slips.

Buckingham's yacht wasn't hard to find. It was taller and
longer than any sailing vessel I could see. And on its stern in
fancy letters was the name:

Golden Hinde
HONOLULU

I craned my neck to follow its mast up to the sky, and had to grab a handrail to steady myself. I wondered how many mom-and-pop Hawaiʻi investors it took to pay the gold dealer's yacht club dues and to stock his boat with caviar and champagne.

"Kai Cooke!" Buckingham waved me onto the spotless deck, then offered his meaty right hand. I almost cut myself on his diamond ring. We sat on cushioned seats in the cockpit as two twenty-something guys in white shorts and polo shirts busily checked rigging and sails. Buckingham told me that he and his wife had sailed single-handedly from Bora Bora to Honolulu. Now with only his daughter's help, and state-of-the-art electronics and auto pilot, he claimed he could still navigate to any number of remote Pacific islands. And when the trade winds went slack, a Cummins turbo diesel kept her chugging at ten knots per hour—plus.

"Nice boat," I said to get the conversation rolling. "With a fitting name."

"The *Golden Hinde* was commanded by Sir Francis Drake," Buckingham replied, "a fearless explorer who circumnavigated the globe for his country and queen."

"Why do I remember Drake as a pirate?" I said, recalling AP history at Flintridge Prep. "Didn't he pillage and plunder along the way?"

"Nonsense. Your American schoolbooks gave you a distorted view of history. Drake was a great man."

I said, "Yes, sir," and let it go.

Buckingham then reminisced about the exotic South Pacific. "Now Bora Bora," he said, "that's what Hawaiʻi *used* to be—but is no more. Paradise."

I nodded politely and then updated him on my efforts to find Kula, mentioning the lead I was following that night. "A Waimānalo man named Moku claims to have Kula," I said. "I thought you should know, sir."

"Too right!" Buckingham hauled out his Aussie talk again and embraced his daughter who had come up from below and sat next to him. It was the first time I had seen her smile.

"I'm not sure how right, sir." I straightened in my seat. "This Moku asked me to bring the entire reward to a dead-end road in the valley at night."

"Don't trust the bloke?"

"Not sure." I gave my client the particulars of the phone call and of the plan for the meeting. Buckingham listened attentively.

"I doubt Moku will bring Kula tonight," I added. "But he may know something about his disappearance. All I can do is go see what happens."

"I'll go with you," Buckingham replied. "You could be in danger."

"That's very generous, but he insisted I come alone." I tried to reassure him. "I'm experienced enough with these kinds of meetings to not put myself at risk. If I didn't think I could walk out alive, I wouldn't walk in."

"Be careful, then." He looked genuinely concerned.

"I will, sir. As I mentioned, the man wants the thousand-dollar reward up front in cash."

"Do you want it now?" Buckingham reached for his wallet.

"Uh, no . . ." I should have known he'd have that much cash on him. "I'd rather not carry it with me tonight . . . until I check out the lead."

"No worries. Ring me on my mobile."

One of the guys in white shorts signaled Buckingham that the *Golden Hinde* was ready to go.

"Sure you won't join us for a sunset sail, Mr. Cooke?" he asked. "We're waiting on one guest and then we're off."

"No thanks. I've got my appointment tonight. I'll call you with any news."

As I stepped from the boat, I noticed a lifeguard surfboard with a red cross on it and the word RESCUE. As big as a tandem board with two pair of handles on the rails, it was mounted on the dock across from Buckingham's slip. Seeing that word made me wish I had some sort of backup that night—but not Barry Buckingham. I was wary of him as a client, let alone as a partner to cover my back.

When I pulled away from the yacht club I saw Madison's Lexus convertible whiz by in a gold blur. Her fingers were tapping the glowing ash of a cigarette into the wind. She didn't notice me. When I glanced back, her taillights were disappearing behind the club's automatic gate marked: MEMBERS ONLY.

eighteen

Waimānalo is a sleepy seaside town in windward Oʻahu, sandwiched between Kailua to the north and Makapuʻu Point to the south. Kapu Road winds deep into an isolated valley behind the town. *Kapu* means "forbidden" in Hawaiian and it's no place you'd want to meet a stranger on a dark night. Especially a stranger who expects you to be carrying a thousand bucks.

Waimānalo's tiny business district fills barely two blocks along narrow Kalanianaʻole Highway. At night there isn't much to see. Ken's In & Out Plate Lunch was closed. So were Shima's Market, Waimānalo Feed Supply, Kuni's Auto & Towing, and Glenn's Nursery. But the lights were still on at Jack in the Box and the Waimānalo 76. And in the distance the jagged ridgeline of the Koʻolau mountains, jutting a thousand feet from the valley floor, was backlit by the lights of Honolulu. In their foothills I hoped to find a clue about the missing dog.

At the one and only traffic light in Waimānalo's commercial hub, I swung a sharp right onto Kapu Road and headed into the valley. An occasional streetlamp poured a pool of light onto the black pavement. But most of the landscape was shrouded in darkness under the moonless sky. The eerie glow of city lights above the Koʻolau range only served to deepen that darkness.

I reached over and touched my surfboard, the nine-six's duckbill nose resting comfortably on the Impala's padded dash. The board, for some reason, reassured me . . . made me feel confident I would live to surf tomorrow. For safety's sake, I'd brought only one hundred and change from my client's retainer. If Moku had information to offer, he'd have to settle for that for now. And if he actually had the dog, a quick call to Buckingham could produce the full reward.

Soon the pavement ended and I started kicking up dust, driving the dirt road until it stopped at a barrier. My headlights illuminated a bullet-riddled sign: DEAD END. Beyond the sign lay a small clearing among the trees. I turned my car around facing back toward the village. When I switched off my headlights, the scene faded to black.

I checked my watch: 10:54.

The high-pitched hum of crickets added to the eerie atmosphere. Eleven came and went. I got out of my car and, with the penlight on my keychain, felt my way with my feet to the clearing. But there was nothing to see, even if I could have seen better.

Suddenly behind the DEAD END sign I heard rustling. I pulled my .357 magnum from the right front pocket of my khakis and stepped beyond the barrier. No, I don't have a license to carry a concealed weapon. But sometimes, when the situation calls for it, I do what I have to do. The sound led back into the underbrush. Probably a mongoose skittering across dry leaves. Then I heard a vehicle rattle up to the dead end and stop. Doors opened and slammed shut. Voices sounded and then I heard the shuffle of feet.

As I crept back toward my car, I saw what looked like an old Honda with its lights on, pulled up beside mine. I could barely make out the two large men who were lifting my surfboard out of my car, and a third, the largest of the three, rifling through my glove compartment. I pointed my gun at them and stepped into the headlights' glare.

"Put the board back."

The men halted then slowly began pushing the board back into my car.

"And get your hands out of that glove compartment," I said. "Which one of you is Moku?"

"Me, brah," said the biggest one.

"You nevah come alone, Moku—like you tol' me. An' I no can see da dog."

"I goin' get da dog. You get da money?"

"Firs' da dog." I kept the .357 pointed at them.

"I get 'em fo' you, brah," Moku said. "Five hundert now, five hundert wen I get 'em."

"Nah, I pay in full when you delivah. How I know you got da dog? Or dat you geev' 'em to me?"

He reached into his pants pocket and pulled out a dog collar. "Is his."

"Les see 'em."

"Five hundert, brah."

"No way. I geev' fifty, if fo' real."

"One hundert," he said. "Or no collah an' no dog."

I pulled five twenties from my wallet and pointed to an imaginary spot in front of me. "Drop 'em hea."

Moku walked up. His dark eyes studied me. Around his neck hung a shark tooth on a black cord. He got close enough that I could see an *M* etched on the tooth in scrimshaw. So *M* is for Moku? I almost said. He held out the collar. It was tanned and stitched leather and had gold-embossed letters that said *KULA*.

The real thing? I had to believe it. This crew didn't strike me as smart enough to make a fake of this quality.

"Try drop 'em." I pointed to the ground with the revolver. "Den take da money."

Moku did as I said and then walked back to his friends. He seemed used to doing business at gunpoint.

"Now you bring da dog," I said.

"Latahs." Moku kept walking. His friends followed him to their car. Not one of them looked back as the old Honda started with a plume of smoke and sped away.

nineteen

Friday morning I was looking into the accusing eyes of homicide Detective Frank Fernandez. Moku Taliaferro was dead. His shark's tooth necklace was missing. And I was suspect number one.

I had no alibi. I had pulled a gun on Moku. The case of the missing dog was turning grim.

"Whose dog is it?" Fernandez asked, impatience in his gravelly voice.

"That's confidential—you know that. Besides, what do you care? It's a dog, Frank."

He scowled.

"What about Moku's pals?" I said. "One or both of them could have killed him for the hundred bucks I handed over."

Fernandez looked incredulous. "Murder—for a hundred bucks? Anyway, they both have alibis."

"Maybe they're lying."

"Maybe." His eyes hardened. "Maybe you are, too."

"C'mon, Frank."

"Tell me your client's name."

"I can't."

"Then next time we'll be talking in my office," he said. "If I didn't know you we'd be there now."

My door had not yet closed behind Fernandez when I began to wonder why I was risking a murder rap to protect a client whose character—and wallet—was suspect. But I believed in client confidentiality. Should it disappear just because I questioned a man's integrity or his ability to pay?

My phone rang, interrupting my thoughts.

"Surfing Detective," I answered.

"If you like fine dat missing dog," whispered a female voice, "try go look in Lanikai. Address is one-o-seven Mokulama. Da druggies dere steal any kine, even one dog. Spock fo' yo'self." She hung up.

I checked the phone—she had blocked her caller ID. I had to keep following every lead, even the questionable ones. The case wasn't just about a missing dog anymore.

Before leaving I called Lou, the Mililani puppy mill owner who had promised me a male blond golden retriever. He sounded too much like Kula to ignore. Was the dog for real? Lou's phone rang. No answer. No machine.

* * *

Soon I found myself driving over the Pali again. From Kailua Beach Park I took meandering 'A'alapapa Drive, along the backdrop of the sheer Ka'iwa Ridge, into the beachside enclave of Lanikai. Only a few days ago I had plastered five hundred posters along this drive. But today the first pole I passed was naked. Next pole, no poster. Another pole, same thing.

Instead of turning onto Mokulama Drive, I drove the entire Lanikai loop that encircles the small community, from the mountains to the sea. Every poster was gone. This was obviously not the work of kids or irritated neighbors because posters advertising lawn sales and missing property were still hanging.

So I wasn't feeling optimistic as I pulled up to 107 Moku-lama. The sagging frame house stood on a narrow overgrown lot half a block from the beach—a plantation shack among glitzy McMansions. A half dozen neglected coconut palms bulged with nuts ready to drop. Beneath each tree were mounds of nuts and fronds where they had crashed. Broken windows, loose shingles, flaking paint, wild hedges, and junk cars on the brown grass screamed neglect.

I parked across the street, surprised that the old hovel looked so familiar. Then I remembered. It had been featured on the evening news—an example of a growing drug problem in the islands and the frustration of citizens trying to combat it.

The owner of the home was a destitute widower in his seventies who had invited some questionable friends to occupy his digs, rent-free, in exchange for improving the property. Most had arrest records as long as their needle-tracked arms. The improvements never happened. Soon it became clear, to his neighbors anyway, that his shack had been taken over by drug dealers, thieves, and prostitutes. So why did he let them stay? The prostitutes. He was fond of them.

His cozy arrangement went along fine until his neighbors—weary of the endless partying and brawling—dialed 911. Even after several busts, the party continued, which is possibly why I got my tip. But why would druggies steal a dog? To feed their habit?

A Doberman sleeping among the weeds darted after me when he heard my car door slam. His fangs sent me back into the cockpit. The Dobie jumped up against my driver's door, his hot breath fogging the window. His claws dug into the turquoise paint.

"Ikaika, ovah heah!" A woman of about forty with dirt-brown hair ratted up into a topknot stepped from the house.

Ikaika turned tail and retreated. The topknot woman chained him under a sagging carport. I stepped from my car and approached her. Up close, I could see a nasty scar zigzagging across her sweaty forehead and dark shadows under her eyes.

"What you want, brah?" Her voice was flat and lifeless.

"I looking for one dog." I pulled out Kula's photo—and my pidgin.

"You wen' put up da signs?" she asked.

"Yeah. You wen' take 'em down?"

"Nah. Why I like take 'em down fo'?" she asked. "You one cop?"

"Private investigatah. Dere's one reward fo' da dog. One t'ousand dollahs."

"I know who wen' take da signs." Suddenly she sounded interested.

"Who?"

"Worth somet'ing, yeah?" She held out her right hand.

"How much?" I asked.

"Hundred."

"Can replace da signs fo' less than dat."

"Fifty, den." She eyed me warily.

I opened my wallet and pulled out my last twenty. I held it up to her intense gaze.

Her eyes locked on Alexander Hamilton's chiseled face for an instant and then she grabbed the bill from my hand. "Moku."

"Moku Taliaferro?"

She nodded.

I didn't bother to poke around any longer at 107 Moku-lama. If Kula was there, would she have settled so quickly for a twenty?

I also didn't bother to tell her Moku was dead.

twenty

Instead of getting back into my car, I walked down Mokulama Drive *makai,* or toward the ocean, to a sand path lined with ironwoods. At the end of the path was Lanikai Beach. In the distance I saw the iconic Mokulua Islands—twin pyramids on the turquoise sea. Heat waves coming up from the beach made the famous islands shimmer. Postcard perfect. I planted my backside in the warm sand, pulled Maile's card from my wallet, and punched in her number on my cell.

"Kai?" She sounded concerned. "Anything wrong?"

"Your cats are fine. How's Utah?"

"The workshop is good. And your investigation?"

"Not so good. A suspect wound up dead last night. His skull was crushed."

"Oh!" The surprise in her voice traveled across the miles. "That's rare in a pet theft case. New territory for me."

"Swell."

"Do you think he was your man?"

"I think he took down every poster I put up about Kula's disappearance."

"Posters are usually taken by people who don't want the pet found, or who want the reward all to themselves. But killing somebody is, well . . . unusual." Maile was silent a moment.

"The more I dig into this case," I said, "the more I think it's not about Kula at all.

"Then who?"

"Maybe Cheyenne Sin—Buckingham's missing wife? Her disappearance has been bugging me from the start. I think Kula is just a pawn."

"A living, breathing pawn," Maile said, "with high stakes to find him."

"What I can't figure is why was Moku killed? I doubt he could be more than a bit player, hardly worth the risk . . ."

"Maybe he's the key to the whole thing," Maile replied.

"Why did I ever take this case?"

"Because you're a sucker for cold noses and warm hearts?"

That phrase again. I had used it on Fernandez. Now Maile used it on me.

"Kai?"

"Sorry, Maile. See you at the airport on Sunday," I said, ending the call. There was no point in telling her the truth—I had taken the case to save my business. No other lofty motives, let alone cold noses and warm hearts.

* * *

Back at my office later that day I played a new phone message:

"Ah foun' yur retriever, boy, an' Ah fur dam shore dezarve that-thar reward . . ." A pause. "Whut yu waitin' fur, boy?" Silence. "Boy? . . . Boy?"

The caller spoke in a drunken redneck twang, not common in the islands. He hung up without giving a number. But he did leave his caller ID.

Strange. A 775- prefix. He had called from the Big Island. Why would someone on the Big Island call about a dog lost on O'ahu?

I called him back.

"Sammy Bob," he answered, this time without the slur.

"Mr. Bob?" I picked up on his cue.

"Name's Picket—Sammy Bob Picket," he corrected me. "Whut kin ah do fer yah?"

"I'm George, and I'm looking for a dog." The name sounded plausible enough, especially on short notice.

"How're yu, George?" He perked up. "Yah dun called the rite place, boy. Whut kine ah dog yah look'n fur?"

"Not sure. What kind do you have?"

"Ah got all kine."

"Golden retrievers?" I knew I was pushing my luck, but hoped he'd forgotten his drunken call to my number.

"Got 'em."

"Are you a dog breeder?"

"Nah, but ah sells 'em, an' ah sells 'em cheap."

"Where are you?" I pushed my luck again.

"Yah doan got tah worry nun 'bout that-thar," he said evasively. "Ah deliver."

"I'd like to see your goldens before I buy one. Can I come and look?"

"Yah got five-six hundert?"

"For the right dog," I said.

"Tell yah what yah gonna do . . ."

I held my breath.

"Yah drive on up the Hāmākua Coast till yah get tah Laupāhoehoe, then yah call me. Ah'll lead yah from there."

"Where will you meet me?"

"Locals Only Café . . . " He paused. "How 'bout tomorrow afternoon?"

"Suits me." I would have agreed to anything.

"Remembah, George, yah ain't gonna get no better deal."

"See you tomorrow then."

"Muchablige." He hung up.

twenty-one

The next morning I caught a 10:50 flight to Hilo, still wondering why a guy on the Big Island would call about a dog lost on Oʻahu. His good-ol'-boy lingo and name also made me wonder.

The airplane to Hilo was packed with weekend travelers on neighbor island getaways. *Holoholo.* Looking out the window as the Hawaiian jet descended south along the Big Island's Hāmākua Coast, I saw the rustic tin roofs of Hilo town nestled along the waterfront, just as I remembered them. Over the years I've watched Hilo sink into the economic doldrums when the sugar industry tanked, and then rise again when tourism transformed the quiet hamlet into a New Age mecca of artsy shops, health food stores, and trendy restaurants. In addition to tourism, the island's recent economy depended on diversified agriculture, not the least of which included illegal cash crops like *pakalolo.*

* * *

After picking up a car at Budget, I drove to Kea'au, about ten miles south of Hilo. There the road climbs southwest into Volcanoes National Park or due south to Lava Tree State Monument. The south road continues to the former seaside village of Kalapana and its famous black sand beach, both devastated by lava flows. Kea'au, on higher ground, escaped.

Once a sugar plantation town on the slopes of the Kīlauea Volcano, Kea'au has since grown into a suburb of Hilo, boasting a Sure Save market, Ace Hardware, McDonald's, Pizza Hut, and a couple of gas stations and churches. I wasn't looking for pizza or religion in Kea'au. I came to find the Hawai'i Island Humane Society shelter, one of three on the Big Island.

The Kea'au shelter was a one-story, hollow tile, tin-roofed building with detached cathouse and dog kennels—all spotlessly clean. Its utilitarian appearance was softened by spacious green lawns, a few palms and an 'ulu, or breadfruit tree. The place had a cozy, campus-like feel.

Inside the facility I explained to a staffer named Alana, whose lava-black hair flowed down to her shoulders, that I was looking for a golden retriever lost on O'ahu. She said she'd do all she could to help.

Pet hoarders—people who gather and even steal large numbers of animals—were a problem in the area, Alana told me. They accumulated so many pets that they couldn't care for them properly and were usually prosecuted under animal cruelty statutes.

"Dis old lady bin keep mo' den one hundred cats." Alana started to "talk story" in pidgin. "Her neighbors, dey smell da stink and dey call. So we go check 'em out. Da cats bin starving. Dey living in one dump. Unsanitary, yeah? Most of 'em really sick. Some dead awready. We bring all da live cats hea. And da old lady get arrested and go to jail. Cruelty to animals."

"You know dis' guy Sammy Bob Picket?" I asked.

"Sammy who?"

"Picket," I said. "He live in Laupāhoehoe. Maybe he one dog hoarder?"

"I hear of some guy like dat. But never hear of dis Picket."

"Maybe he da same guy?"

"Maybe," she said.

Before I left, Alana told me that another animal control officer had heard rumors of a dog hoarder on the Hāmākua Coast who'd been stealing animals from shelters at Kona and Waimea. But this operator was different. He didn't just steal and hoard pets, he sold them to hunters of pig and wild boar, and to trainers of fighting dogs. The hoarder was a traumatized Gulf War veteran who drifted to Hawai'i after the war and never left. How he had ended up, years later, stealing dogs on the Big Island, no one knew.

It sounded to me like Picket might match the profile of this trafficker in stolen pets.

"I go check 'em out." I headed for the door.

Alana replied, "Maybe he *lolo.*" By which she meant crazy.

"Maybe." I waved goodbye.

"Be careful," she called after me.

* * *

I pulled away from the shelter and drove up the windward coast. A half dozen seaside villages drifted by before I reached Laupāhoehoe. At the once-booming sugar town's most famous landmark, Laupāhoehoe Point Park, windswept ironwoods and palms clung to a craggy black point in the turbulent sea. The Point's rugged beauty wasn't speaking to me today. I was heading *mauka,* or inland, in search of a man I didn't really want to meet.

I followed Picket's directions to a fifties-style diner called Locals Only Café. Over the sweetly-sad blare of Ricky Nelson's "Poor Little Fool" on the jukebox, I asked a waitress dressed in a pink carhop outfit where I might find a man named Sammy Bob who sold dogs.

"Oh, *dat* guy." She frowned. "Why you want 'em fo'?"

"I looking for one golden retrievah."

She gave me a curious look and said she only knew general directions—up the sloping land *mauka* off the highway. She'd heard that Picket was hard to find. From the expression on her face and the way she talked about him, I could tell Picket wasn't her friend. In fact, I figured she didn't like the guy. So I wasn't worried she would tip him off that I was coming unannounced.

My plan was not to call and not to link myself with the lost dog. I would just show up as a guy wanting to buy a retriever.

I drove up a narrow blacktop called Manowai'ōpae Homestead Road. It wandered deep into the country until there was nothing but fields and woods on either side of me. The pavement ran out. I turned onto a dirt road and kept wandering, dust kicking up behind my rental car. There was nothing much out there, aside from overgrown cane fields and woods. Even if Picket didn't steal dogs, his seclusion suggested he had something to hide.

Eventually the road turned into a tire-rutted trail and then a dry creek bed. Soon I couldn't even tell if there was a road at all. The woods were thick. I was going into nowhere. I reached instinctively for my Smith & Wesson and then remembered that I hadn't packed it. The hassle of flying inter-island with a handgun.

I was cursing myself for getting lost—maybe I should have called Sammy?—when I saw a shack far off through the trees. I stopped my car in the creek bed and started walking into a jungle. The green canopy grew darker and more tangled. I began to hear dogs whining and smelled the now-familiar odor I'd whiffed at Lou's puppy mill. I hoped the breeze that brought the stink my way would also keep my scent from the dogs' keen noses.

In a clearing a rotting plantation shack stood ringed with trash. Between the shack and me were the remnants of a bonfire and what looked like charred dog collars and blackened tags and licenses. Beyond the shack was dog city. Or dog ghetto. Animals were everywhere: tied to rusted out vehicles, a cast-off refrigerator and stove, and plywood crates. There must have been three-dozen dogs in plain sight and more hidden elsewhere.

I scanned the crowd for Kula, keeping far enough away and out of sight to avoid the barking frenzy that I knew would erupt if I was sniffed or spotted. None of the dogs even remotely resembled Kula. If any were purebreds, I couldn't tell. The animals were skin and bones. Some faintly resembled breeds I'd seen before, but their emaciated bodies and mangy fur rendered them all pitifully alike.

Before that moment I couldn't have imagined animals in worse condition than those at Lou's puppy mill. But here they were, staring me in the face. I'd never been an animal rights advocate, but scenes like these might make me one. And more were coming.

Staked close to the shack were two bony pit bulls tied with leather leads. Their jaws were huge. One was white with a black spot and the other tan. Their pale yellow eyes reminded me of the tiger shark that attacked me at Laniākea. I must have gotten too close because, suddenly, their big jaws gaped, their lips curled, and out came their teeth. The leather straps tightened with a frightened snap. *Attack mode.* Pit bulls sometimes get a bad rap for being predators, but this pair seemed worthy of the reputation.

As the two dogs pulled and snarled, the shack's door flew open and a man stepped out with a double-barrel shotgun.

"Whut n' hell . . ." He pointed the shotgun at me.

I froze. He was the embodiment of the redneck voice I'd heard on the phone: stringy gray hair, greasy beard, scabby limbs scorched by the sun, cigarette dangling from his lower lip.

"Listen up. Ah gonna shoot yah ass, whoever yah are . . ." He sighted down both barrels.

twenty-two

"Don't shoot, Sammy Bob . . ." I tried to calm him. "It's me, George."

"George who?"

"I called yesterday. You said you'd show me some dogs."

"Dang-it, George." He lowered his shotgun. "Ah tol' yah to call me from the café. Doan yah remember nothin'? How n' hell did yah fine me?"

"I asked in town. Somebody said you were up here, so I just drove." I stepped into the clearing as he walked toward me. The stink coming off him was nearly as strong as the stink of his dogs.

"Alright, George." He scratched his greasy hair to help himself remember. "You was look'n for a golden retriever, right?"

I nodded.

"Ah kin give ya a better deal then them pet stores, or them fancy high-priced breeders. You jus' come with me. Ah gonna put mah gun in the house. You doan gotta worry none. Jus' come with me."

He set his shotgun inside the door and led me back toward the cobbled kennels. On the way we walked by the two pit bulls, who went ballistic. I jumped back. Their leather straps snapped so tight again I thought they'd break. I'd have preferred chains.

"Stay back! They'll take ya hand off," Picket said. "Ah otta know." He held up his left hand, whose middle finger was missing above the first knuckle. "Them dang pit bulls hate everybody, ah tell you. They'd eat me alive, if ah let 'em loose."

"Why do you keep them around?" I was curious.

"Good question, George. You'd a thunk ah'd kilt 'em awready. But ah can't. Them's worth too dang much money as fight'n dogs." He chuckled. "If they doan kill me firs'."

"So where are your retrievers?" I scanned the makeshift kennels.

"Ah doan keep my goldens out here. No way, boy. Them there dogs is fer hunt'n an' fight'n. Or fer folks that gotta hanker'n to et 'em. Nah, ya doan wan' none of them."

He turned us around and walked to the door of his shack. "Come on in, hear?" He motioned me to follow.

His shack was no larger than my Waikīkī studio apartment. Now I'm not the tidiest housekeeper, but Sammy Bob didn't bother at all. Trash was everywhere, piled up to heights that would make even Mililani Lou green with envy. But he didn't go in for rum like she did. His drink of choice was Kentucky bourbon. Empty quart bottles seemed to float like ghost ships on the sea of litter that was his floor. Maybe that's what he'd been drinking when he first called me. Anyway, his place reeked like something had crawled inside and died.

"Wanna smoke?"

I shook my head as he lit a cigarette. The shack filled with smoke; there wasn't much ventilation. I looked up and saw two tiny holes in the roof to which the smoke ascended. He then led me to an adjoining room, no more than a closet, where a half dozen animals were curled up on newspapers.

"This here's some purebreds, George. Them's nice dogs."

When I looked in, the animals cowered. A skeletal black creature that might have been a Labrador glanced up at me fearfully. Another with the brown and black markings of a Rottweiler squealed faintly. The rest hardly moved a muscle. I couldn't tell if they were drugged or traumatized or just weak from lack of food, water and fresh air. I tried to pet the black dog, but he recoiled from me.

That feeling of revulsion I had had looking at his outdoor dogs came back again. Only stronger. I wanted to turn away, but didn't.

"I don't see a golden here," I said.

"Hold on, George. Thought ya might like to see that-thar nice lab. Goldens is in the nex' room."

Picket slid open a door to a group of smaller animals. I saw what looked like a mangy Maltese, a dirty cocker spaniel with cheerless eyes, and a toy poodle with long, matted hair. Another sad sight. I tried not to show Picket what I was feeling.

"Nah, nex' room." He opened a third door to the bathroom. "Now, this here's what ya look'n fer, George. I gots two. Take yer pick for six hundert. Cash and carry, boy."

On the grungy floor curled up around a toilet and pedestal sink were two golden retrievers—thin and dull brown. Both lay unnaturally still. Compared to the photo of Kula, those famished animals looked like victims of a concentration camp—a Dachau for dogs. It made me sadder than sad. But I tried not to show it.

"These two are dark," I said. "Do you have a light-colored one?"

"Dang-it, boy!" Picket slapped his thigh. "If yah'da been here the other day. Ah got the nicest, sunniest golden retriever ya ever seed. This here dog was a beaut, ah tell you."

"That sounds like the dog I want." I tried not to appear too anxious. "Where is he?"

"Ah ain't suppose to say. Ya know how it is."

I reached for my wallet. "Sammy Bob, I know you're an honest businessman—a man of integrity." I watched his scabby face take on a proud look. "And I know you wouldn't betray your customer, but if he or she was to sell me this dog, I would cut you in. Say, two hundred?"

"Boy, trouble is, ya doan know where to look."

"Half the commission up front," I sweetened the deal. "One hundred now. One hundred when the sale goes through."

"OK, George, tell ya what ah gonna do." He stroked his beard. "Ah gonna tell ya where to go. But ah want all the money up front. All two hundert in cash."

"I haven't got it with me." I opened my wallet for him to see—four twenties, one ten, one five, and several ones.

He thought it over. "Ya gonna pay me the other hundert when ya buy that-thar dog?"

"Yes." I knew I wouldn't and he probably knew I wouldn't, but we had to go through the charade for his self-respect.

I reached into my wallet and gathered up the bills. "Here's the money." I held it in front of him.

He snatched the bills from my hand. "Georgie boy, you gotta fly Maui, then drive to Lahaina."

"Lahaina?"

"One of them big houses on the ocean. Now there's lots of condos on the beach, but there ain't that many oceanfront homes. So ya should find it easy." He walked back out to the main room.

"Do you have a name? An address?"

"Ah plum forget, George." Picket put on a sincere face. Then he casually reached over and rested his hand on his shotgun, where it leaned inside the doorway.

"Well, if you remember, call me." I gave him my home number—the answering machine there did not mention my name.

As I turned to leave his shack, I asked, "What's going to happen to those goldens? And all those dogs outside?"

"Ah gonna fine 'em good homes." He flashed a smile. "Ah does a good business."

The pit bulls snarled at me as I passed. Whines and howls of other captives followed me all the way back to the car. I was glad to get away. But I felt a tug of conscience with each step I took.

Turn him in, a voice inside me said. *Turn him in.*

But I couldn't yet, not until I found Kula. And to do that, I might have to call on Sammy Bob Picket again.

twenty-three

As my Maui-bound plane lifted off over Hilo Bay I congratulated myself that the famous surfing dog might be waiting for me in Lahaina. But why would anyone go to the trouble and expense to ship a stolen dog to several different islands? I wondered again what was really behind the case. A missing person? Murder? Even more puzzling to me was what made a hoarder like Sammy Bob Picket, or puppy mill owner like Lou, mistreat animals. It reminded me—sadly—of an episode from my small kid time in Hawai'i.

* * *

Before my parents died, my father thought it would be a good idea for my dog Pono to be obedience trained—to learn to heel, sit, and lie down on command. Since I was too young to take him to class alone, my father and I went together. The trainer was a rigid, severe woman of the old school who got very physical with the dogs. I saw her once yank a tiny terrier off its feet with a choke chain. When the terrier yelped instead of obeying, the trainer's corrections got even more physical. I covered my eyes.

One day it was Pono's turn. The trainer commanded "Down!" Pono, of course, had no idea what to do. Then she yanked him south so hard that Pono flopped onto the ground. He got back up. The trainer commanded "Down!" again. He didn't. She yanked harder. Pono flipped over and whimpered. The corrections continued.

I ran to him and covered his trembling body with mine. "Stop hurting Pono!"

My father gently peeled me off the dog. "Kai, this is how Pono will learn to obey."

"I don't care if he obeys," I cried.

I saw my father and the trainer exchanged glances.

We never came back to that class. And ever since that day, whenever I see someone abusing an animal I remember Pono and I feel like I should *do* something. So I couldn't agree more with Maile—people who harm helpless creatures are the lowest of the low. Pono's trainer was not in the same league with Sammy Bob or Lou, but in my childhood memories she was just as bad.

* * *

At Kahului Airport, I slipped into my second rental car of the day and headed for the historic whaling port of Lahaina, on West Maui's leeward coast. It was already late in the day and carloads of tourists and *kamaʻaina* commuters were making the slow trek west on seaside Honoapiʻilani Highway, also known as Route 30, that leads beyond Lahaina to the resorts of Kāʻanapali and Kapalua. Needless to say, the highway was jammed.

Sitting in traffic, I wondered if I'd make it to Lahaina before sundown. Otherwise, I'd have to wander around in the dark looking for an oceanfront home for which Sammy Bob had refused to give an address. I thought again about his starving animals. Well-fed and well-groomed dogs would bring more on the open market. So why keep them in such horrible shape? Was Picket a sad story like Lou's husband—wounded by war? Or was he simply depraved?

I finally reached Lahaina town just after 6:00 p.m. I pulled into a service station and checked a Maui phone directory for veterinary clinics. There was only one in Lahaina. Good news. But would the clinic be open at this hour? I hoped so. I wanted to avoid the added time and expense of spending the night in Lahaina, unless it was absolutely necessary. Plus, the sooner I made contact with Kula, the sooner I could close the case.

I dialed and waited three rings. "Lahaina Animal Clinic," a perky receptionist answered. "This is Caitlin."

"Hi, I'm a member of the Golden Retriever Club," I launched into an elaborate lie, "and I'm following up on an adoption. Has a golden retriever—male, about three years old, light in color—been brought in for a checkup in the last few days?"

"He has," she said with certainty. "What a gorgeous animal! And I assure you," she continued, "Boomer received the best medical care."

Boomer? "I'm sure he did. And so I'm wondering if you can help me. I'm on my way to visit Boomer in his new home, but I've lost the house number. I thought you might have it."

She hesitated. "Well, I do. But our policy . . ."

"I understand," I said. "It's just that I drove all the way from Upcountry and I haven't been able to reach the owner by phone. I thought I had the right number, but . . ."I paused. "It's getting so late—I hate to turn around and go all the way back."

"Well," she said, "I'm sure Mrs. Varda wouldn't mind . . ."

* * *

Armed with Mrs. Varda's address and phone number I drove north along Front Street, watching the sun sink over Lahaina town. The bars and eateries on the bustling seaside strip were hopping. But farther up the beach, where posh oceanfront homes nestled peacefully on the shore, you could hear trade winds whispering in the palms and shore break lapping the sand.

Like most seaside residences in this pricy neighborhood, Mrs. Varda's resembled a walled fortress from the street. Two identical garages with separate driveways stood at the extreme ends of her property. Their windows revealed a Jaguar convertible inside one and a pewter Mercedes inside the other. Between the garages ran a high lava rock wall and an even higher grove of areca palms. Even if Kula had become the mascot of this lavish estate, there was no seeing him, or anything, from my vantage point.

I walked down a nearby beach access to get a glimpse of the place from the water: two stories with a tile roof in china-blue. The ocean side was all glass, glowing in the setting sun. I could see no one inside the house or outside on the grounds, which included a kidney-shaped swimming pool, lounge chairs, chaises, potted palms, and a putting green. No one was swimming in the pool either. Only a yellow tennis ball floated in the water.

A mock orange hedge with a teak gate surrounded the beach side of the property, but the hedge was not so high that I couldn't peek over. Nice place. But no dog in sight.

I called his name: "Kula."

A minute passed.

I called again.

It was going to get dark soon. I was running out of time.

Then it happened. From behind a palm, where I guess he'd been napping, the golden retriever dove into the pool—*Splash!*—and swam after the tennis ball. Even half-swallowed by his own wake, his blond coat was unmistakable. He was alone, but he kept looking around, as if to see who'd called his name.

"Kula," I tried again."

He glanced my way with those vivid brown eyes. The contrast between the eyes and his almost white face was striking. The photos hadn't done him justice. He was every bit as stunning as Buckingham had said. I could see why someone might want to steal him.

Kula climbed from the pool and walked toward me. His tail flicked water every which way. His gold fur dripped on the deck. His gleaming white teeth clenched the yellow ball.

When he reached the gate he shook, drenching everything in sight, including me. His wagging tail picked up speed.

Then he barked. Not an aggressive bark. A social bark. But loud.

"Shh . . . Kula . . ."

A glass door in the house slid open and out stepped one of those wealthy middle-aged women whose bleached hair and perpetual smile look plastered in place.

I crouched behind the hedge.

"Boomer?" Mrs. Varda strolled on the pool deck. "Boomer-boy!"

The golden retriever, hearing his new name so soon after the old, looked suddenly confused. He tilted his head, peered at me, and then trotted back toward the house. He stopped before reaching Mrs. Varda and shook again. She draped a big beach towel over him and tenderly patted his damp coat.

"Does Boomer-boy like swimming in Nanah's pool?" Out came the baby talk. "Oh, yes, he does! Oh, yes he does!" She was in love.

Kula glanced back toward the hedge.

I did not approach Mrs. Varda. Whether she was unaware that the dog she purchased had been stolen or she was part of the scheme, she wasn't about to hand him over to a strange man popping up from behind her hedge. Not likely at all.

To do this job right I needed a pet recovery expert. I knew just the one. But she was in Utah at the moment. The liberation of the famous surfing dog would have to wait for another day.

twenty-four

As the setting sun silhouetted the island of Lāna'i like a humpback whale cruising across the channel, I hopped in my rental and drove back to Kahului Airport. By 8:40 I was airborne to Honolulu. By 10:00 I was in Mānoa feeding the cats. I wished Maile was there so I could tell her the good news.

Same drill as before. While Coconut and Peppah devoured their dinners in the kitchen, I catered to Lolo again on my hands and knees under Maile's bed. I felt slightly guilty about feeding the felines at such an hour, but apparently they were fine. And Maile would never know.

When I pulled away thirty minutes later I was feeling on top of the world. My first and only pet case was almost closed and I had hopes the fee would carry me until my next case—a real one with people. Not dogs and the scum that abuse them. It was too late to call Buckingham. The good news would have to wait until morning.

Then, as I drove down East Mānoa Road, I had second thoughts. Yes, I'd finally found Kula, and, yes, I could trace his disappearance back to Sammy Bob on the Big Island. But how had the retriever gotten there? Was Picket involved somehow in Moku Taliaferro's murder? And in Cheyenne Sin's disappearance?

* * *

Back at the Waikīkī Edgewater, I had two phone messages, the first from Madison: "Kai, Conrad called again from L.A." She was talking fast. "I think he suspects something."

Usually the essence of cool, Madison seldom showed concern about anything, let alone her husband. Even Twinkie was yipping frantically in the background.

"I'm sure it's only a bluff," Madison hurried on, "but Conrad says he's flying to Honolulu . . . *Twinkie, hush!*"

I skipped ahead to the second message: "Don't make me come after you, Kai," Detective Fernandez growled. "You've got two choices. Tell me who you're working for or I'm bringing you in for Moku's murder. I'll give you the weekend. I better hear from you by Monday."

* * *

Frank Fernandez's voice was still ringing in my ears when I woke up Sunday morning. I had a feeling of dread. One day left to give Fernandez an answer.

After breakfast it was still too early to call Buckingham, so I phoned Maile. It was about noon then in Utah and I imagined her workshop took Sundays off.

"Kai," she answered on the first ring, "How are you?"

"Well," I said, happy to hear her voice.

"And how are you getting on with the cats?"

"Peppah glommed on to me right away, Coconut barely blinked, and Lolo ran for cover."

"You described them to a tee."

"And how's your workshop?"

"Fantastic," she said. "I'm learning so much about animal sanctuaries, no-kill shelters, and stuff like that. Well worth the trip."

"That's good . . ." I hesitated. "Good."

"Is there something wrong, Kai?"

"Wrong? No. I just wanted to tell you the good news."

"What good news?"

"Remember Kula?"

"How could I forget that beautiful retriever?"

"Thanks to your advice, I found him."

"Brilliant, Kai! I'm so glad."

"Yes, it's a bit of a miracle, really."

"Congratulations."

"Thanks . . . uh . . . I should call my client, now that it's a decent hour here. Lehua is going to be jumping with joy."

"I'm sure she will," Maile said.

I had an inspiration. "Why don't we go out and celebrate when you get back?"

She was quiet for a moment. My knees suddenly felt weak. I found myself blurting out: "What do you say, Maile?"

"Sure, Kai, I'd like that."

"Excellent," I said. "After all, it was you who told me how to find Kula."

"I was glad to help."

"Okay, I better call Buckingham." I said. "See you soon."

"I'll look forward." she said.

When she hung up I realized that I had neglected to tell her that while I had found Kula, I hadn't actually brought him home. And that I needed her help for that. A small detail that could wait for her return.

* * *

Still glowing from Maile's congratulations, I prepared myself mentally for the barrage of thanks and attaboys I would soon receive from my client. I dialed Buckingham's Tantalus mansion.

"Good news, sir," I said. "I located your dog."

Buckingham didn't say a word.

"I'm sure your daughter will be very happy," I added.

"Why don't you pop up here, Mr. Cooke." There was a ragged edge to his velvet voice I hadn't heard before. "I have something to tell you that I'd rather not discuss on the phone."

My sense of dread returned. "I'll be right there."

* * *

Weaving up Tantalus Drive I wasn't so much wondering about Buckingham's strange tone, as I was recalling Mrs. Gum's allegation that he had killed his wife. And that shadowy face in a second floor window, ducking behind a curtain when our eyes met. Were my client's tone and the mysterious figure connected some way? Now I was really grabbing at straws.

I pulled to the curb in front of Mrs. Gum's colonial, walked across the street to Wonderview, and was buzzed through. Buckingham himself, without his daughter this time, met me at his dark *koa* doors, appearing as bleak as he had sounded on the phone. Even his three-piece suit, the same shade of charcoal he had worn at our first interview, did not soften his desperation.

"Mr. Cooke, there is something we must discuss." The edginess I had heard on the phone now sounded close to panic, the way people talk just before they lose it.

He led me into his sunken living room. I sat while he paced in front of the ocean-view glass, his dark figure a somber contrast to the sunlit sea below. Lehua still had not appeared.

"I asked you to come here, Mr. Cooke, because there is something I have to tell you that I didn't want to say on the phone."

"Is it about your golden retriever, sir?" I was still hoping for that cash reward, plus my fee. "I'll have Kula home to you shortly."

"You've done a superb job finding my daughter's pet. Superb. I wonder, though, if you have discovered *why* her dog was stolen."

"Why, sir?" I was taken aback by this unexpected question. "You hired me to find the dog, not the thief's motives."

"Right you are, Mr. Cooke. You've done your job and, I assure you, you will be rewarded." Before he got to specifics about my money, Buckingham appeared to think better of it and shifted direction. "But at present I have another problem that's more in your usual line."

"Another problem?" W*hat now?*

He paused and stared down at the sea. "My daughter's gone missing."

"Your daughter, sir?"

"She failed to return home from summer school Friday and I haven't seen her since," Buckingham said.

"Almost two days have gone by?" I was stunned he'd waited so long to tell me. "You must have called HPD?"

The gold dealer stopped directly in front of me, blocking the sun. "I'm a very public man, Mr. Cooke, and my reputation is essential to my business. My radio audience must have complete confidence in me or my business will wane. And as you can probably imagine, with a place like this," he gestured to his sprawling mansion, "I have to keep the money rolling in. No, I don't intend to call the police."

Not even to save his own daughter?

"I'm giving you a new case. Lehua has been kidnapped. That you found Kula so quickly makes me confident that you can also find her."

"You're sure someone has abducted her—she's not just gone AWOL like a typical teenager?" I asked. "Have you checked with her friends?"

"I can assure you, I have called all of her friends, including the few boys she has dated. She is with none of them. Her Mini was towed early Saturday morning. It had been illegally parked on Wilder Avenue."

"How do you know she was kidnapped?"

"The same man who abducted my wife and her dog has now taken my daughter."

"Do you mean the prowler, sir? Has he contacted you?"

Buckingham ran his fingers though the red roots of his black hair. "There is more I have to tell you . . ."

twenty-five

"About twenty-five years ago," began Buckingham, "down in Australia, there was a bloke named Abe Scanlon, a con man who ran a rather successful Ponzi scheme—desert land in the outback. He sold the worthless land to city dwellers who never bothered to inspect their investments. Abe promised them income each month from rent." Buckingham cleared his throat. "He got them their money—by luring in new investors. Meanwhile he was skimming off the top for himself."

"Abe Scanlon is the prowler?" I tried to make a connection to his daughter's disappearance. And maybe his wife's.

"I'll get to that." Buckingham sat across from me. He put his hands together against his chin, as if in prayer.

"He has something to do with it, then?" I pulled out my pad and pen.

"I can assure you . . ." Buckingham looked at me with his pale blue eyes. "He does."

I wrote down the name: Abe Scanlon.

"Abe wasn't much of a front man, you see," the gold dealer continued. "He had the face of a mule, thinning hair, and his voice was shrill as a bird. But then I came along. My name was Billy Brighton then."

I wrote below Scanlon's name: Billy Brighton.

"I was young then." Buckingham smiled. "Handsome, if I do say so myself. Red-headed, rough, and ready for anything. I had trained to be an actor in Sydney, then when things didn't work out in that line I took to the sea. I sailed the world. It was a tough life. I survived a few brawls in faraway ports. It was every bloke for himself. And some didn't survive. Luckily I was good with my hands . . ."

"You had to kill to survive?" I looked again at his hands and the gold rings that adorned them. Neither those rings nor the walnut-sized diamond perched on one of them could conceal the hugeness of his hands. Recalling his vice-like grip I concluded he could snap a man's or woman's neck with the ease of a nutcracker.

"I would never admit to that." Buckingham glanced at the faded quilts on the wall behind us. "Anyway, we're getting a bit off course."

"Not a problem." I looked at my pad. Two names so far: Abe Scanlon. Billy Brighton.

"Main thing, I had what Abe didn't. A voice. A handshake. A physical presence. I could inspire confidence. He saw my potential. I could make him money. Lots of money."

"So Scanlon hired you?"

"Of course. He wasn't stupid." Buckingham ran his fingers through his hair again. "With me aboard, Abe's business flourished. He paid me well enough for an apprentice, but I couldn't help seeing the torrent of cash flowing into his pockets. And I couldn't help seeing his glamorous wife—who later became my wife."

"Cheyenne Sin?"

He nodded. "She was a fashion model—far younger than Scanlon. Cheyenne was in her twenties like me and regretted marrying old Abe for his money."

"So that's how the two of you hooked up?"

"We were instantly attracted. She was a beautiful woman. Still is. But something else bonded us."

"And that was?"

"Scanlon's Ponzi scheme fell apart. The pool of gullible investors shrank. Rent payments dried up. Scanlon danced around the problem by relying on me, but investors complained. Some sued."

"Bad news."

"I saw what was coming and convinced Cheyenne to come with me to New Zealand. We took what assets we could, anything that wasn't bolted down."

"I bet Scanlon didn't like that."

"It was too late for him, mate. He got arrested."

"And you and Cheyenne took off?"

"We felt the heat, I'll tell you. So we bought a sloop and sailed to Bora Bora. We lived there unnoticed for awhile, but hardly in the style Cheyenne was accustomed to."

"So you moved again?"

"When Scanlon was convicted and thrown in prison in New South Wales, we rechristened our sloop *Golden Hinde* and sailed to Honolulu. I changed my name, for obvious reasons, from Billy Brighton to Barry Buckingham. I colored my hair. I took to wearing three-piece suits. A sort of makeover."

"Sort of." He made it sound like a small thing—changing his identity and appearance to evade the law.

"In Honolulu I went into the precious metals business, where my acting skills helped me launch my radio program, *Gold Standard.*"

"And that's how you bought this place?" I gestured to the sunken living room, one of countless rooms in his hilltop estate.

Buckingham flashed a self-satisfied smile. "It was amazing how quickly it happened."

"An overnight success?"

"You could say that. We needed lots of cash. Wonderview didn't come cheap. And then Cheyenne gave birth to our daughter, Lehua, and suddenly we were a family."

"So what about Abe Scanlon?" I asked. "Is he still in jail."

Buckingham arched his brows. "Afraid not. That's why I'm telling you this. It may sound strange to you, but . . . "

"No, sir. Continue." His story did sound strange, but I wasn't about to agree with him.

"Back in New South Wales, after serving twenty years for fraud and tax evasion, Abe got paroled. The poor man had lost everything—his fortune, his work, his wife. He'd become a bitter old man. And he blamed me, of course."

I was about to say, "I can see why." But kept it to myself.

"Once Abe was released from prison, his only thought was to find me and my wife and make us pay. In my view, he has only himself to blame. But that didn't stop him."

"So he's here? Scanlon is in Hawai'i?"

Buckingham returned to his prayerful pose. "Unfortunately yes."

"Not good." I raised my own brows.

"Abe searched the Pacific Islands for Cheyenne and me with no luck, until one day during a stopover in Honolulu he heard my voice on the radio. He dialed the number I gave on the air and threatened to turn us in to Australian authorities."

"Blackmail?"

"Exactly. He had argued in court that Cheyenne and I were equally to blame, but since we disappeared, they had only Abe to try."

"Has he made any attempt on your life?"

"Murder wouldn't have accomplished what Abe wanted: to take my life apart piece by piece."

"You're sure about that?"

"If Abe kills me, he gets nothing. He can't milk me dry unless I'm alive. Don't you see?"

It was my turn to nod.

"But Abe's demands for cash got out of hand—beyond my ability to pay. That's when Cheyenne disappeared. Then Kula. And now Lehua. So you see, Mr. Cooke, he's behind all my misfortunes."

"And you're sure he's turned from blackmailer to kidnapper?"

"No doubt." Buckingham pulled out a handwritten note:

> *Do not doubt my resolve, Billy. If you want to see your daughter alive again, put fifty thousand in cash into a briefcase and await further instructions.*
> *Your old partner*

"Has he given you the instructions?"

"This evening at midnight. Sand Island," Buckingham explained. "He wants me to stop at the chained gate leading to the park. I'm to come alone."

"You should definitely not go alone, sir. You don't want to jeopardize Lehua's life. . . . or yours. I'll go with you."

Buckingham sighed. "Fine," he said. "Meet me back here at eleven. Do you have a gun?"

"Yes."

"Bring it.

twenty-six

I re-crossed Tantalus Drive that Sunday morning wishing I had never set foot in Wonderview. I've had my share of sleazy clients, and the smooth-talking gold dealer was quickly rising to the top of the list. But I feared for his daughter, who had nothing to do with her father's crooked past. And I wondered why there was no ransom note for his wife—if Scanlon had in fact abducted her. And why Kula had ended up on Maui.

Walking to my Impala, I saw Mrs. Gum standing at her mailbox. Her silver hair was shining in the morning sun like the figurine on Buckingham's Rolls.

"Good morning, Mr. Cooke," said the widow.

"Ho, you have one excellent memory, Mrs. Gum! You remembah my name." I tucked in my aloha shirt which had come loose after sitting with Buckingham

"I remembah 'cause I need to tell you how he did 'em."

"How who did what?"

"How Mr. Buckingham *make* his wife."

"How did he do 'em, Mrs. Gum?" I played along, but by now was almost ready to believe her.

"He wen' strangle her an' den dump her body into da ocean from his sailboat. Das why da police no can fine her. Da sharks eat her."

"So why Mr. Buckingham want to *make* his wife?"

"To collect her life insurance. He wen' sell her Bentley car only two weeks aftah she disappear. Dat doan tell you somet'ing?"

"Maybe he need da money."

"Of course. Dey argue ovah money all da time. Das why he *make* her."

I thanked Mrs. Gum for her help and wondered about her sanity. And mine. I had agreed to meet another shady character in some deserted spot in the middle of the night. The repercussions of my last meeting were still haunting me—in the form of Detective Frank Fernandez, who seemed way too eager to put me behind bars.

* * *

Winding down Tantalus Drive, I passed the street where Dr. Carreras had lived before his vintage Porsche flew off the road into a tree. I remembered his calling Buckingham a fraud and then promising to tell me things that would make me want to drop him as a client. After the gold dealer's recital about his past, and Mrs. Gum's repeated allegations of murder, I found myself wishing, now even more, to know what Dr. Carreras might have said.

I looked down to the ocean. Off in the distance a south swell was steaming in at Ala Moana "Bowls." Later the crowds would be out. But in the morning, even on a Sunday, a persistent surfer can usually find an open wave.

That decided it. My nine-six riding beside me in the car, I aimed down the hill to Ala Moana Beach Park, slipped off my khakis down to my board shorts, and paddled out. The south swell was kicking up into a nice hollow left, the way they sometimes do in summer. The waves were shoulder high and rising. But was I wrong about the crowds! Surf city.

I didn't wait long. A set of three good ones popped up on the horizon. The first one came and was packed with riders. I let it go by. The second one was packed too. By the third wave the crowd thinned. I caught it. The green wall swept left and peaked. I stepped to the nose, crouched, and set my arms wide. I was flying, brah. *Flying.* The world suddenly contracted into that single moment. I thought of nothing but the wave . . . the ride.

Surfing has a way of easing my cares, of leaving them back on shore where they belong. But I didn't entirely forget the case. In the lull between sets I thought about Barry Buckingham (a.k.a. Billy Brighton) and his missing dog and daughter and wife. I thought about his blackmailer—Abe Scanlon. And I thought about tonight's handoff at Sand Island.

Kidnapping doesn't leave many options. The ace up the sleeve is always the hostage. The kidnapper can threaten to harm unless conditions are met. Usually a ransom. Even meeting his conditions doesn't guarantee the hostage's safe return. I hoped the smooth-talking Buckingham could talk his way through this one. But if he couldn't, I'd better have a backup plan.

* * *

Later that day I picked up Maile at the airport. It kills me how airlines announce arrival times in hours and minutes, like

12:05 and 10:13. As if the schedule is so precise you could set your watch by it. I have never known an airplane to arrive exactly on time. But so as not to stand her up, I pulled into Honolulu International well before 2:04 that Sunday afternoon. Because of the beefed-up security after 9/11, I had to wait in the windowless cellar of baggage claim. No food. No shops. No amenities except rest rooms. Just when you thought air travel couldn't get worse, it did. Mercifully, Maile's flight from Salt Lake City via San Francisco had caught a tailwind and was early.

Arriving passengers began making their way down an escalator and through sliding glass doors that led to baggage claim. I watched bedraggled adults and half as many boisterous kids stream in, keeping an eye out for Maile. Before long she stepped through the doors in denims and a peach-colored T-shirt that said "Best Friends," beneath the likeness of a doe-eyed puppy. Even at a distance I could see an aura around Maile. I found myself wondering why I'd ever lost touch with her.

"Kai!" Maile hugged me. "Thanks for coming."

Her sweet scent reminded me of Mrs. Fujiyama's *lei. Lei!* What an idiot! I'd forgotten one for Maile. But she didn't seem to notice. She hugged me like the old friends we were, rather than like a fellow detective. That was all right with me.

"So when do we go out and celebrate?" Maile asked.

"Well . . ." I said sheepishly. "I have a favor to ask."

"What's the favor?" Maile looked curious.

"I found Kula," I tried to explain. "Yes I did. Thanks to you . . ."

"That's fantastic, Kai," she said. "But you told me already on the phone . . . Remember?"

"Yeah, I remember. But what I forgot to tell you is . . ."

I was interrupted by an airline announcement: "Passengers on flight ninety-three from San Francisco can claim their baggage on carousel H-four. Please note that many bags look alike . . ."

"You forgot to tell me what?" Maile looked puzzled as passengers swarmed the carousel behind us. A red light flashed, a foghorn-like beeper sounded, and the carousel clattered into operation. We turned and watched the first pieces of luggage bounce down and start their slow circular journey.

"I found Kula, but . . ." I struggled on, "I didn't bring him home."

"Why not?" Her brows knit.

"Kula's on Maui. He was stolen, just as you predicted. Then sold to a woman who owns an oceanfront place in Lahaina. I went there, cased out the property, and spotted Kula. But I couldn't see how to take him without setting off alarm bells. I didn't want to botch the job, so . . ."

"So what?" She shrugged her shoulders.

"Truth is, Maile, I need a pet recovery expert. What do you say?"

Maile didn't miss a beat. "When do we go to Maui?"

"Then you'll do it?"

"No problem." She put her hands on her hips in mock gesture. "But you're still going to take me out to celebrate, right?"

"Definitely. How about tonight?" Then I remembered my date with Madison.

"Uh . . ." she hesitated. "Let's wait till we bring Kula home. Anyway, I haven't seen my cats for days. I better go spend some time with them."

I was relieved, but only said: "When will you be ready for Kula?"

"How about Tuesday?" Maile asked. "That will give us one day to prepare. We'll need a few things: A large dog carrier, plus evidence that Kula belongs to your client—AKC papers

or a license. And it would help to have someone with us Kula
knows well and will come to. How about the girl?"

"I'll ask Buckingham." Lehua's kidnapping and the sordid
history behind it was too long to tell Maile just then.

"You know, Kai, the right way to do this would be to inform
HPD that Kula was stolen. Your client could file a police report
then."

"He won't."

"Okay . . . I guess. So we can get Kula home and he can deal
with the legalities later."

"My client's not much for legalities."

Maile glanced at the carousel. "There's my bag!" She pointed
to a plaid cloth suitcase.

I rushed to the carousel and snatched it.

"Thanks." She smiled. "We make a good team."

I should have warned her: I almost never work with a partner. I had my reasons, but kept them to myself.

twenty-seven

After dropping Maile off that afternoon, I swung by my Maunakea Street office. Inside the flower shop Mrs. Fujiyama was ringing up a customer with a white ginger *lei*. The sweet-spicy aroma followed me up the orange shag stairs to my door.

The fact that I'd already found Kula didn't stop people from calling. Only Maile, Buckingham, and I knew. I fielded five messages: Two desperate pet owners pleaded with me to find their missing Chihuahua and Airedale. A third caller asked me to train her to search for lost cats. A fourth had actually spotted a light-colored retriever, but by now I knew it couldn't be Kula. And a fifth asked if anyone had claimed the $1,000 reward.

Still no real cases. Had I been pegged as a pet detective?

* * *

When I went home to dress for dinner, another message awaited: "Georgie, now doan yah let me down, boy."

Sammy Bob Picket's twang was unmistakable.

"Remember, yah owe me another hundert when yah git that golden. Jus' put it in the mail, general delivery. Or bring it by now."

* * *

Madison sat at her usual oceanfront table when I arrived for dinner that night at the Waikīkī Canoe Club. Her cigarette, martini, and cell phone were all going—Maltese in her lap. Her cherry hair fell darkly to her shoulders. When I saw her I felt a mix of emotions. But one clear thought: we had to break it off.

Maybe Tommy was right. Maybe I *was* lonely. Or maybe loneliness was just an excuse—a smokescreen for the undeniable fact that Madison was somebody else's wife. Even if her husband was almost never around.

Then there was my old friend Maile—confident and wise enough to be just who she was: tough and independent. Yet she had a soft spot for animals and people in need. Luckily, that had always included me. I couldn't help but wonder what she was doing at that moment.

I took a chair. Twinkie leaped from Madison's lap into mine and planted her wet nose against my crotch. Madison snapped her cell phone shut.

"Twinkie! Show some restraint, girl!"

I pushed the dog's nose away.

"Did I tell you, darling," Madison flicked her cigarette ash into the tray, "that I decided to buy gold from Barry Buckingham?"

"No." I tried not to show concern. "Is that who you were on the phone with?"

"Of course not." Madison laughed. "Have you found Barry's dog yet?"

"Still working on it." I didn't want to jeopardize Kula's rescue. Not after all I'd gone through to find him. And the truth was, I wasn't really sure I could trust Madison.

"Enough about him. Conrad's still threatening to fly to Hawai'i, you know, but he doesn't say when. How can I plan my life?"

"Have you ever thought of divorce?" I asked, and then wished I hadn't.

"If I divorced Conrad, I'd get nothing. His lawyers would see to that." She took a drag from her cigarette. "Can you imagine me economizing at my age?"

"You're not even forty, Madison. And you look barely thirty." It was a politic thing to say—and true. But she wouldn't stay young long if she kept that pace of smoking and drinking.

Her face brightened. "You're a gentleman, Kai. That's why I keep you around."

The cocktail waitress approached and Madison pointed to her now-empty martini glass. "The same," she said.

* * *

After a Canoe Club burger for me and lobster bisque and scallops for Madison, she invited me to her penthouse for a nightcap. I told her I had a case to work that night.

"If you don't want to be with me," she snapped, "don't make excuses."

"It's not an excuse, Madison. I do have a case."

"Well, would you at least walk Twinkie and me home?"

We both knew what that meant. Once again, I found myself saying yes. We stood, she kissed me, and I felt a familiar rush.

* * *

When we arrived at her swanky Diamond Head apartment building, I noticed a limo leaving the garage with personalized plates that started with H. The long black Lincoln pulled away before I could read the rest of the plate. We rode the elevator to the top floor and walked the carpeted hall to her penthouse. Madison slipped in her key and turned the knob.

"That's odd," she said. "It's not locked."

"Are you sure?" I tried the key myself.

"What if somebody's in there, Kai?"

"I'll go first." I pushed open the door and stepped into the dim, sprawling apartment, Twinkie at my heels.

Someone walked toward me. Madison reached for my hand. Twinkie recoiled in fear.

A bald portly man in a satin robe and carrying a highball said: "Dear?" He spoke in a soprano that seemed at odds with his bulk.

"Conrad . . ." Madison hesitated a moment. "What a surprise. When did you get in?" She dropped my hand and put her arms around his substantial self.

"Just ten minutes ago," he said. "I had one of our resort cars drop me off. I wanted to surprise you."

That vanity plate I had spotted on the limo probably said HIGHCAMP.

"Conrad," she giggled, a little too loudly. "Oh, darling, this is a private detective." Madison pointed to me. "I didn't want to worry you, but someone has been stalking me. So I hired Kai Cooke here. I heard he's *very* good."

"Kai," he shook my hand, "the pleasure is mine."

"Mr. Highcamp," I said, "it's an honor to meet you, sir. Mrs. Highcamp has told me all about you." It was a lame thing to say, but the best I could come up with at the moment.

"That so?" He shrugged and then laughed. "Now listen, Kai, I want you to send your bill to me personally. Will you do that?"

"Yes, sir."

"Call me Conrad," he said. "Madison will give you my address in Los Angeles. She can be a little tightfisted, as I guess you know." He winked at me. "I'll expect a statement at the end of the month."

"Right, sir." I handed him one of my cards. "In case you need to get in touch with me."

He took it.

"Well, you two no doubt have a lot to catch up on," I kept talking. "Mrs. Highcamp, you probably won't be needing my services now that Mr. Highcamp is in town. But if I can assist you in the future, please give me a call."

"I'll do that, Mr. Cooke," she said with distant politeness, but I doubted her husband was buying it. I sensed that he knew what she was up to.

I turned on my heels and walked to the elevator. By the time it reached the ground floor I decided that this would be my last date with Madison Highcamp.

twenty-eight

When I met Buckingham later that night at Wonderview, he looked more like a mugger than a millionaire. No charcoal suit and ruby tie. Instead, black sweats, sneakers, and a wool cap pulled over his brows. His ruddy face looked ashen, his blue eyes eerily pale. Was this Billy Brighton, the sailor who'd stolen his partner's fortune and bride?

Buckingham led me into his living room overlooking the lights of Honolulu. He walked to a bookcase and from behind a row of gilt volumes—more for show than reading—he drew a snub-nosed pistol. He fingered it for a moment and then tucked it into a pocket in his sweats.

"Have you heard any more from Scanlon?" I asked.

"Nothing."

"Did you get the cash?"

Buckingham gestured to a leather briefcase on the Berber carpet—monogrammed in gold, B.B.—and consulted his Rolex. "It's almost eleven thirty. Shouldn't we be going?"

"Let's talk through what we're going to do first," I said.

"Yes, good idea." He seemed relieved to have me there to work out logistics.

"We'll take your car, since Scanlon is expecting you alone. I'll ride in the backseat and stay out of sight. When we reach Sand Island, we'll wait by the gate for his call. Scanlon will probably want you to carry the briefcase to a drop point. If he does, I'll shadow you. If anything goes wrong, I'll move in."

"No heroics, Mr. Cooke. This is my daughter."

"I only want to protect you and your daughter, if she's actually there."

"If she isn't, I won't leave the money," Buckingham insisted.

"Of course." I tried to calm him.

"Let's be off then." His ashen face showed a determination he might need before the night was over.

I followed Buckingham through his rambling villa to an attached three-car garage, past his daughter's mint green Mini and the empty space once occupied by his wife's Bentley, to his red Rolls. Atop its mile-long hood stood that silver figurine and beneath that his vanity plate: GLD DLR. Whoever was waiting for us could never miss this car.

I climbed into the back and sank into parchment leather. The smell of the hides was strong. Buckingham pulled away and wound down the darkened road. His briefcase rode next to me in the back seat.

As he negotiated the last few turns on lower Tantalus Drive, the gold dealer turned back to me and said out of the blue, "Like my Rolls?"

"Yes, sir, it's very nice."

"*Nice?*" He said in his pitchman's voice, his confidence clearly returning. "This car cost me more than your average man's home. But I'm not your average man. Am I?"

"Definitely not, sir."

It was a strange thing for him to say, dressed as he was like a hoodlum and, stranger yet, on his way to ransom his daughter. I wondered how many average men's life savings had gone to buy his Rolls. And what price his wife and only child would ultimately pay.

"I'm not being boastful, you see." He shrugged. "Just proud. I built my business from scratch. Nobody gave me anything."

Nobody but Abe Scanlon, I thought. *And as many people as you could sucker along the way.* But who was I to cast stones? I was working for the man!

When we turned onto Nimitz Highway, I wondered about the resourcefulness of our opponent. Was it likely that the old man would return Lehua for the briefcase? And what about Cheyenne? A blackmailer usually wants more. I didn't picture the old man tossing any grenades, but I didn't doubt he might enlist some muscle who would.

As Buckingham hung a left into Sand Island Access Road and crossed the bridge, a container ship slipped silently from Honolulu Harbor, its illuminated rigging resembling strands of Christmas lights. Sand Island sat in the middle of the harbor, leaving only the narrow channel for the ship to pass through. The beach park rimmed the south shore of the mile-and-a-half long island, where we were soon stopped by a chain across the entrance.

I'd been to Sand Island Beach Park in the daylight. It's a tranquil spot to grill burgers and tilt back a few beers. But at two minutes to midnight the park was black. That there was only one road in made me wonder about Scanlon's plans. I could not imagine an old man alone restraining a kidnap victim and collecting a ransom at the same time.

At midnight Buckingham's cell phone rang.

"Yes, just like you asked for . . ." He took a deep breath. "Abe, it's all there. But I have to see my daughter first." There was a long pause. "I'm on my way."

Buckingham whispered to me in the backseat. "He wants me to carry the briefcase into the park. He'll call me again near the drop point. He still hasn't told me where it is."

What was Scanlon's game? Although his criminal history had been nonviolent, as far as I knew, I was growing increasingly uncomfortable with what he might have planned for his late-night rendezvous with his former partner.

"If you don't like what you hear or see once you get there," I said to Buckingham, "tell Scanlon to wait and come back to the car. I'll meet you here."

"Right."

Buckingham stepped out of the car. I gave him a few seconds' lead and then followed behind. In the dark park he was nearly invisible in his black sweats, toting his briefcase. We walked less than twenty feet when his cell phone rang again.

He talked animatedly into his phone, but I couldn't hear what he was saying. Soon he walked to a nearby trash bin and carefully balanced the briefcase on the rim. Then he rushed back toward his car.

Already he was veering from the plan.

I ducked behind a tree as he walked by, keeping an eye on the briefcase. Buckingham's cell phone rang again. He was close enough to me this time that I could hear him clearly.

"Yes. Yes. I kept my end of it. Now you keep yours."

He put away the phone and walked back to the Rolls, opened the door, and slid into the driver's seat. I stayed out of sight, waiting for Scanlon to emerge from the darkness. Buckingham continued to sit in his car.

What was he doing?

Nearly ten minutes passed. No more phone calls. No sign of Lehua.

About to leave my post, I was stopped by a movement near the briefcase. From the shadows appeared the bent outline of an old man. I couldn't say he was running, he seemed incapable of that. But he was walking as fast as someone his age could—a halting, awkward gait.

Just as Scanlon reached the prize, Buckingham's door opened. I saw three quick flashes and heard *pop-pop-pop*. I couldn't tell if the old man was hit. He grabbed the briefcase and hobbled away.

Then in the darkness, somewhere behind where Scanlon had been, there were two more flashes and pops. Somebody was firing back!

I ran to the car. Buckingham was leaning against the open door, holding his snub-nose.

twenty-nine

"I trust I hit him," Buckingham said calmly. "I trust I hit Abe at least once."

"Get in," I said. "Let's get out of here."

Buckingham slid back into the driver's seat and closed his door. I jumped in the backseat. He turned the Rolls around and left Sand Island Beach Park behind. I looked through the back window, but saw no more flashes coming from the park.

"Who was that with the gun?" I asked. "It wasn't Scanlon. He was too busy with your briefcase."

"I don't know," Buckingham said. "I also assumed Abe had compatriots, but have never myself come face-to-face with one."

"You shouldn't have fired." I was furious. "You could have hit your daughter. Not to mention me."

"Lehua wasn't here." Buckingham slumped back into the seat. "He said she would meet me at the car if I left my briefcase on the bin. Damn him . . ."

"And now he has your daughter and your money."

"Well, not exactly, Mr. Cooke." A smile crossed his face. "I filled the briefcase with old newspapers. This was a little cat and mouse game, you see, between Abe and me. Abe had hoped to fleece me for another fifty thousand, and I had hoped to kill him. Neither one of us succeeded tonight, but there will be other nights, believe me."

"But your daughter . . . and your wife."

"Nothing means more to Abe Scanlon than money. If he harms Lehua or Cheyenne, he's lost his meal tickets."

"So you think he has your wife too?" I recalled Mrs. Gum's very different version of events.

"Of course. It's the only explanation for her disappearance."

"Then why no ransom note?"

"Abe is twisting the sword in me. He wants me to suffer. The note will come—when he's ready."

Just as I realized there was no sense in arguing with him about Scanlon's motives, Buckingham's cell phone rang again. He kept his hands on the wheel. He didn't answer.

"Abe wants to shame me," he said, "but I won't give him the satisfaction. He is not a man of honor."

Did Buckingham think of himself as honorable?

"Mr. Cooke," he cleared his throat, reclaiming his usual pompousness, "since Abe cannot be counted on, and my family's life is still at stake, I'd like to defer to your expertise at this point."

I looked in disbelief at the actor-sailor-turned-pitchman who just this morning told me his history of swindling others. Even if I didn't hate working for a crook who would throw me the sort of curveball he just had—what kind of miracle did he expect me to perform? What on earth made him think that I could find a way to get the girl from Scanlon, especially after Buckingham himself had just spooked the man with a double cross and an attempt on his life? Then I thought of Lehua and the danger she was in.

"Well," I sighed, "my fee just doubled."

"Agreed."

"First let's see if we can intercept Scanlon. We might be able to catch him on the access road, unless he's gone by boat."

I had Buckingham pull off the road after about a half mile behind a big Matson truck. He shut down the motor. In less than five minutes we saw a pair of headlights. He started his Rolls again and grabbed the wheel.

"Wait," I said. "If that's Scanlon, we need to follow him at a distance."

The headlights got bigger and soon an SUV appeared. It fit the description of the vehicle that the elderly *tutu* I'd interviewed on Kailua Beach thought she saw Kula riding in. I could see two people inside as it passed: a man hunched in the backseat, and a man wearing a baseball cap driving. Soon the SUV's taillights faded into two tiny red dots.

"Keep your headlights off," I said. "And follow him. Stay about a quarter mile back."

As we crept along in darkness Scanlon's driver turned from the isolated road onto the more heavily-trafficked Nimitz Highway. They were heading west, toward Pearl Harbor. Buckingham switched his lights back on as we entered the ramp onto the H-1.

Freeway lights revealed the SUV to be a bronze Chevy Tahoe. As the road made its sharp bend near Aloha Stadium, the Tahoe merged into the far right lane. When the H-3 Kāneʻohe exit approached, the Tahoe's right blinker came on and it took the ramp.

"Is he going back to the scene of the crime?" I wondered aloud.

Buckingham said nothing. He seemed focused on Scanlon's taillights.

The Tahoe climbed the H-3 grade to its summit and then descended through the tunnel toward Kāneʻohe and Kailua. At the Kailua ramp, they pulled off and aimed straight for Kailua town. Before long the SUV swung into a side street and then into the driveway that led past the auto parts store to the Windward Sands.

"Spyder Silva," I said. "And Reiko Infante."

Buckingham didn't react to the names.

"I've been here before," I added.

The Windward Sands looked less seedy at night than when daylight revealed its cracked windows and rotting wood. But more eerie. Flickering TVs glowed from inside through open jalousies, emitting the ghostly noise of disembodied voices. While Buckingham parked his Rolls out of sight by the auto parts store, I walked along the overgrown hedge flanking the property and positioned myself where I could see and not be seen.

The driver of the Tahoe hopped out and waited for Scanlon. Though his face was hidden by the bill of his baseball cap, I could see tattoos on Spyder Silva's arms. In his right hand was the Berretta pistol I'd seen in his truck.

"There's our shooter," I said under my breath.

Scanlon struggled from the backseat. The absence of blood on his clothes showed he hadn't been hit by Buckingham's wild firing. Then from behind the back seat another passenger got out.

Silva took the girl's bare arm with his left hand—pistol still in his right—and led her into the Windward Sands.

Lehua.

thirty

Buckingham tiptoed up to me like a two-hundred pound ballerina, wool cap pulled over his brows.

"Scanlon's inside the apartment," I said. "And Spyder Silva. And . . . Lehua."

"Lehua?" He reached into his sweats for his snub-nose.

Before I could respond we saw the blue light of a police cruiser turning into the alley. Buckingham's snub-nose disappeared back into his sweats. The cruiser pulled up, stopped, and the officer got out. He took a good long look at Buckingham. If the officer recognized him, as he could hardly help doing, he was discreet enough not to ask why Hawai'i's most famous pitchman was out at this hour dressed the way he was.

"May I see your ID, sir?" he said to Buckingham. Then he turned to me. "You too."

After we handed over identification, the officer got back into his car. His fingers danced on the keyboard of a laptop mounted above the transmission hump. He studied images on the screen. I wondered if Detective Fernandez had put out an APB on me.

The officer then got out of his car and handed our licenses back. "You have a good evening, gentlemen." He nodded and turned away. I guess I hadn't yet made HPD's most wanted list.

I waited until the blue light on the cruiser disappeared down the street before turning back to Buckingham. The situation had become too dicey for me to follow through on my first impulse. It didn't take me long to decide—as I usually do—that working without the help of law enforcement was the better choice. We would get Lehua out of there ourselves.

"Here's the plan," I said. "We'll wait for Scanlon and the others to go to sleep. I'll go in and you'll stay in the car ready to haul us out of here. Turn it around so you're facing the street. When I come out with Lehua, we'll need to hurry."

"But shouldn't I go with—"

"We have to do this right," I cut him off. "We can't risk another incident like at Sand Island. She could be in the crossfire this time."

"But—"

"Silva has a Berretta and he's already used it. He's who was firing back at you."

"Right, then." The pitchman seemed reconciled. He returned to his car and turned it around toward the street. I sat with him in the Rolls for awhile and then walked back toward the Windward Sands. Silva's corner apartment had two outside walls, with high jalousie windows. They were open wide on that warm night.

A distant streetlight cast a faint glow against the glass. I stretched to peek in. The first room was a hollow shoebox except for two single beds. One was empty. The other contained a man whose tattoo-covered arm hung over the sheet. Silva. His Berretta lay on the floor, next to the bed.

The second small room held two beds and two occupants, only their long hair visible on each of their pillows. The carrot-colored hair had to be Lehua's. And the darker, I guessed, was Reiko Infante. It didn't appear that Silva was taking turns with her watching the girl. He'd left that entirely to the one woman in the gang. Or maybe she didn't trust him with the job.

With Silva and Infante accounted for, that left Scanlon. The old man must have been in the living room—sleeping or awake, I could only guess. If I entered through a bedroom window, I could probably exit the front door without much trouble from him. I'd have to hope there were no other accomplices.

I peered through the second bedroom window again. Infante still slept soundly. I began quietly removing slats from the louvered window.

Breaking and entering. I could lose my license. But by the time we could convince HPD that Lehua had been kidnapped— even if her father would agree to that—she might be harmed or taken somewhere we couldn't track her.

After removing the last jalousie I could reach, I saw Lehua move. I couldn't understand how she could sleep after being kidnapped. Infante lay stone-still. A good time to move. I needed to climb up to the window ledge and then hoist myself in. Not easy, alone.

Scanning the dim yard, I spotted an empty planter box a few yards away. Not ideal, but it should work. I got it and flipped it over beneath the open window. Cautiously standing on its edges, I gained just enough height to lift myself up and over the ledge. Rolling down into the room, I stood still, waiting for my eyes to adjust to the dark.

I tried to approach Lehua quietly, to keep her from making a sound. But it was dark, and she couldn't see who I was. She screamed as my hand went to her mouth, muffling the sound. Infante groaned and rolled over, her back to us.

"Lehua, get up," I whispered. "It's Kai. We've got to get you out of here. Now!"

"But my mom," she whispered back in terror. "They'll kill her."

"They don't have your mom," I said. "Let's go." It was a hunch, and seemed to convince the girl.

Noises started coming from elsewhere in the apartment. Either Scanlon or Silva, or both, must have been awakened by our voices. I took Lehua by the arm and started to lead her out of the room. Somebody was coming down the dark hall. I pulled Lehua back behind the bedroom door.

Someone burst into the room. I swung the door into him and saw the old man go down on the floor. I almost felt guilty knocking over the old fellow, until I saw the hatred in his eyes and the kitchen knife in his hand. I kicked the knife across the room.

"Wake up, Spyder!" Scanlon screamed from the floor in a shrill, thin voice that hardly carried beyond the room. "You damn druggie, wake up! Your girlfriend is worthless."

Silva didn't respond. Nor did his girlfriend, though she was only steps away. I didn't bother to point my .357 at Scanlon. He wasn't getting up soon.

"She's not dead, you know." The old man looked up at me.

I glanced at Lehua, then back at Scanlon, and shook my head. "Obviously."

"Not her," he said, "her mother."

"Where is she?" I asked Scanlon, taking a shot in the dark.

Then wished I hadn't. Lehua's eyes started to fill with tears.

"I bloody well don't know," the old man said. "If I did, don't you think I'd've cashed her in by now?"

He had a point. Why kidnap a former wife and then hold her for months on end without trying to gain advantage?

"You want to know where she is, mate?" Scanlon said. "Ask her father." He pointed to Lehua. "He's the one who knows."

Now the girl was crying.

"See yah later." I led her by the arm out of the room, keeping the gun on Scanlon.

Buckingham was waiting in his Rolls. The engine was running. Lehua climbed into the front seat and her father hugged her. She quickly broke free and moved as far from him as she could, huddling against the passenger door.

As Buckingham drove toward Tantalus Drive, he tried to talk to his daughter. She wasn't buying any of it.

thirty-one

It was almost 3 a.m. on Monday morning when I pulled into the Waikīkī Edgewater, rode the elevator to my studio, and fell onto my bed. I didn't undress. But beat as I was, I couldn't get the case out of my mind.

Bringing home the famous surfing dog would close my first (and definitely last) missing pet case, but it would hardly tie up all the loose ends. No way Abe Scanlon would stop blackmailing Buckingham, a.k.a. Billy Brighton. My rescuing his daughter would only make the old man gouge the gold dealer all the more. He had not seen the last of Abe Scanlon.

Then there was Buckingham's missing wife, Cheyenne Sin. According to Scanlon, she was still alive. But had the old man kidnapped her for his ultimate ransom? Or had Buckingham himself, as his neighbor Mrs. Gum alleged, done away with her? I wondered again why he hadn't hired me to find his wife, and instead sent me after his lost dog. And finally there was the crushed skull of Moku Taliaferro—a crime Detective Fernandez was still trying to pin on me.

Kula's disappearance was the tip of the iceberg. But all the rest of it beneath the surface wasn't my job. Once I brought home the golden retriever, Barry Buckingham would have to find another P.I. I was done with him. His rotten side had begun to stink. After collecting my fee, I would say goodbye to Wonderview. Forever.

* * *

My so-called sleep was interrupted by some crack-of-dawn fools drag-racing down Ala Wai Boulevard. I dozed off again until the sun flooding my apartment and the roar of morning traffic forced me out of bed. Still in my street clothes. My aloha shirt had climbed up under my armpits like a life vest. My khakis were so wrinkled I almost tossed them in the trash.

Trying to revive myself, I walked to my closet-sized kitchen and pulled down a package of old-fashioned oats. My parents had New England roots and I can still remember my mother telling me to start the day off right with a good breakfast. To her, that meant hot oatmeal. To me, it was a lot of fuss. Why dirty a pan and wait around for the oats to boil when you could pop open a box of cold cereal? I don't know why I kept oatmeal around. I never ate it. Well, almost never.

I sat a pan on one of my two burners, put in some water and a pinch of salt, and waited till it boiled. Then I put in a cup of oats. And waited some more.

"I might need my strength today," I told myself.

The kitchen steamed up. I got down a spoon and bowl and some honey. My mother used brown sugar, but I didn't have any. Once the oats were cooked, I cover the pan and let them stand, as she used to say. Then I spooned the steaming glop into my bowl.

The first spoonful reminded me how right she was. The oats warmed me all the way down.

The phone rang. I didn't recognize the number. I let the answering machine take it.

"Kai Cooke," said the quavering old Aussie voice, "don't think for a minute, mate, I'll forget or forgive. You are no better than Billy. And your fate will be no better. I know where you live."

How did Scanlon get my number? Did he have my address too? Or was he bluffing? If Buckingham was right, and Scanlon's god was money, my part in last night's adventure couldn't have endeared me to him. One more reason to watch my back.

* * *

At my office there were more phone messages concerning Kula: erroneous sightings, useless tips, and a distraught pet owner begging me to find her beagle. There was also a message from Frank Fernandez—we had reached his Monday deadline. No grizzly-bear mood this time. Teddy-bear instead, which concerned me even more.

"Reiko Infante," Feranadez said. "Remember her, Kai? You tracked her to Kailua on your lost dog case." His tone changed. "She's dead. Somebody climbed through her window last night and smothered her with her own pillow. We're checking for fingerprints, but for now we're holding her boyfriend, Silva. And guess who he says did it? *You* . . . That's two murders connected to you, Kai. Don't make me come get you."

Fingerprints? Mine would be all over Infante's windows and her bedroom. I couldn't call Fernandez right now. If he took me in, I might not come out.

I reluctantly gave Buckingham a call. His voicemail answered. I left a message that I was planning to bring Kula home on Tuesday and asked for the retriever's license and AKC papers. I also asked if Lehua could go with Maile and me. I didn't mention Reiko Infante.

Then I crossed Maunakea Street to C & K Diner and brought back a teriyaki chicken plate lunch to my office. I ate alone at my desk, picking over the chicken with a plastic fork. Until Buckingham returned my call when his radio show ended at four, I was just marking time. And trying to stay clear of Frank Fernandez.

No-brainer. I went surfing.

* * *

At Kaka'ako Waterfront Park, a few blocks from my office, I checked out the edgy break by the Kewalo Channel called Point Panic. The swell was forming into sweet green barrels that rolled about forty yards and then slammed into lava-rock boulders fronting a seawall. A half dozen bodysurfers were carving it up. They milked each wave to its last drop, pulling out a split second before crashing into the rocks. *Daredevils only.*

Point Panic got me thinking again about the case. Though I don't consider myself a daredevil, and seldom panic, I felt as if I were riding a big wave and a wall was coming fast. My gut told me that Buckingham's charcoal suits and black hair were only a surface manifestation of a darkness that lay deeper inside the man. Bad things do happen to good people. But sometimes bad things happen to bad people too. That was Buckingham.

Point Panic—despite its provocative name—was not for longboards. The sign posted by the break reads: Bodysurfing

Only. Board riders there can get arrested. But a short walk *ewa,* near the channel to Honolulu Harbor, leads to a less edgy break called Flies that does welcome the rest of us. Flies produces a mushy right when the swell runs, like today, about knee-to-chest-high. Only four riders were out.

I paddled toward the lineup and hopped on the first wave of an inside set. It fizzled. I paddled farther out and waited. Had I known about Buckingham's history, not even my Impala running on fumes would have made me work for him. Kula, Lehua, and I were all pawns in the chess game he was playing with Scanlon. Not to mention Cheyenne Sin.

* * *

When I returned to my office, Buckingham had left a message. I could pick up Kula's papers at six, but he said nothing about his daughter coming with me. I called Maile and asked, a bit awkwardly, if I could spend the night on her couch. I don't know why I didn't ask Tommy Woo. Tommy lives closer than Maile and I'd sacked out in his place before.

Maile didn't hesitate. "If you don't mind sharing the couch with the cats. . ." She paused. "Well, maybe not Lolo."

"I wouldn't ask," I said, "but the bad guys found out where I live. This case is getting kind of hairy and I don't want anything to stand in the way of our trip tomorrow to Maui." I didn't mention that the good guys now seemed to regard *me* as a bad guy. And they too knew where I lived.

"Whatevah," Maile shrugged it off. "How about dinner?"

"You're sure it's no trouble?" Truth is, a home-cooked meal sounded way good.

"We'll have something simple. How about pasta?"

"Fine. What can I bring?"

"Red wine would be nice," she said.

"Red it is."

Maybe I was wrong, but it sounded like a date.

thirty-two

At a quarter to six I drove once again to the summit of Tantalus.

Buckingham buzzed me through and I climbed the granite steps to his *koa* doors. One swung open and there he stood in his charcoal suit—tie askew. His bloodshot eyes suggested he'd slept even less than I had. He handed me Kula's papers documenting his pedigree and ownership.

"And what about Lehua," I asked. "Can she come with me and my assistant to get Kula?"

"Lehua has just endured a traumatic ordeal, as I'm sure you can imagine. She best stay here . . ."

The way he said this convinced me he hadn't consulted his daughter.

"It may be more difficult without her, but I'll do my best . . ." I paused to gather my thoughts. "There is another way you could help the investigation along. I've already used the retainer you gave me to locate Kula. A second retainer, sir, would help pay for travel expenses to Maui and for Kula's safe return."

The gold dealer winced. "Rest assured, Mr. Cooke"—out came his smooth-as-silk voice—"you will be rewarded handsomely. In addition to your normal fee, I have decided to give you the reward I offered for Kula. You found him. You deserve the reward."

"That's very generous of you, sir. It's just that there will be expenses tomorrow morning that . . ."

"Mr. Cooke"—a dark shadow crossed Buckingham's face—"I have given you $1,000 in advance for Kula's safe return. That's nearly what I paid for him as a puppy. You have located him, so you tell me, but you have yet to bring him home. Now, I trust you are a man of honor, and I trust you believe I am too . . ."

"Of course, sir." I stopped myself from reminding him that I had single-handedly rescued his daughter at considerable risk to myself. For that, he would get a separate bill.

"I will make arrangements to have your check ready when you return with Kula, including the reward." Then he said, "Cheers." The interview was over.

Something told me I would never see that check.

* * *

Driving to Maile's that night for dinner I remembered something that happened the summer I spent in Hawai'i before my senior year. Maile, her boyfriend Karl, and some other friends and I went to a movie. I can't remember what movie or where, but I do remember that Karl and I sat on either side of Maile. It was no coincidence that I sat next to her. Toward the end of the film, as if to punctuate a climatic scene, she put her hand on mine. It seemed like just a playful thing between friends, and it probably meant more to me than it did to her. What did I know? I was seventeen and had never had a girlfriend. I looked over at Karl. He was engrossed in the film. He wasn't paying attention to Maile. Her hand felt warm and seemed to bond to mine. We held hands for I don't know how long. After awhile I got scared and I guess she did too. Our hands went back into our own laps. And Karl was still watching the film.

Maile and I never talked about that time at the theatre. She left with Karl and I didn't see her much again that summer. Funny I should think of this after so many years. Maybe because it was the closet thing to a date I'd had with her before tonight?

* * *

No restaurant in Honolulu ever served a more memorable meal than she did that night in her Mānoa cottage. Homemade pasta. Sauce from scratch. Fresh-baked bread. The supermarket Chianti I brought was hardly up to her cooking, but it put me in a mellow mood. Not to mention the candlelight reflecting in Maile's eyes.

By the end of the meal—a little late—I finally got around to toasting her.

"Of your many talents, this one I like best." I hoisted my wine glass. "Here's to Maile Ohara."

"Barnes," she said.

"Sorry. It just shows you," I said, feeling the wine, "we never know how things will turn out."

She reached both hands across the table, candlelight flickering in her eyes, and took mine. "You weren't here, Kai. You were on the mainland."

"I'd rather have been here. But it's not like I had any say."

"I'm so sorry about your mom and dad. They were such good people. And I know they both adored you."

"I have my memories of them. But I've got to believe my life would have turned out different had they lived."

"How?"

"Well, maybe I'd have stayed in the islands. And maybe the guy you dated in high school would have been me."

"Maybe." She stood and abruptly began clearing the table. "Dessert?"

"If it's half as good as dinner." I followed her into the kitchen.

Maile opened the freezer, removed a stainless container covered with frost, and set it on the counter. Inside, a pale yellow ice gave off a sweet citrus fragrance that stopped me in my tracks.

"Lemon," she said. "Homemade."

That did it. I put my arms around her.

"Are you sure this is what you want?" She looked into my eyes.

"Ever since that summer," I said.

What came next started off shy and innocent, a high school kiss, and slowly grew warmer and more passionate, like the kiss of long-lost lovers.

Next thing I knew, we were in her bed and I was gazing at her naked body. She was just as gorgeous as in her younger photo with her late husband. Slipping off my shirt, I saw the expression on her face. To my surprise, it wasn't shock, but curiosity.

"How'd that happen?" She pointed to the teeth marks on my chest.

"I never told you?"

She shook her head. "I can see we have a lot to catch up on."

"Laniākea." I said. "Probably a tiger shark. But we didn't get well acquainted. He took one bite and swam away."

"Oh," she said and continued to kiss me. "I think I'll have to sample you myself."

thirty-three

Tuesday morning Maile and I flew to Maui wearing sleepy, satisfied smiles. Some passengers aboard the Hawaiian jet may have mistaken us for newlyweds on an island-hopping honeymoon. To be so lucky.

What I felt being with Maile couldn't compare with my experiences with Madison. Nights with her always ended in dark, lonely drives home. With Maile, the sun was always shining.

The airplane's cargo hold carried an extra-large portable kennel for Kula and a small duffle containing the tools of Maile's trade—leashes of various lengths, collars, pet chews and treats, a whistle and clicker, binoculars, pepper spray. I didn't figure we'd need the pepper spray, but Maile said she took it on *every* case. I had booked a return flight that would give us about three hours on the ground in Lahaina.

* * *

At Kahului Airport we rented a minivan roomy enough for the kennel and headed up the coast highway to Lahaina. As the island of Lānaʻi rose on the horizon, Maile turned to me: "Kai, I've recovered a few pets in my time. And I've resorted to some unconventional tactics. There's no predicting how a case will go. We'll just deal with what we find."

"Pet cases and people cases don't sound much different," I said.

"In pet cases, the animals aren't usually the problem. People are."

"Mrs. Varda doesn't strike me as the type," I said. "I wonder if she even knows Kula was stolen."

"Don't kid yourself," Maile replied. "She can't be that naïve. But I don't think we should confront her. It wouldn't guarantee she'd release Kula to us."

"Then why bring his papers?"

"For airport security."

* * *

We parked a few doors from the oceanfront home of Mrs. Varda, our minivan pointing toward Kahului Airport. I led Maile down the beach access to the secluded white sand beach and seaside palaces.

We hid behind some coconut palms in front of the property next to Mrs. Varda's, watching and waiting. A few beach walkers ambled by. No Mrs. Varda. No Kula.

As we sat on the sand under the palms, I noticed our conversation was different now than before last night. Not the words we spoke, but how we spoke them. We weren't the same two people anymore. We had crossed an invisible boundary together from which there was no return. And when our eyes met, they remembered. No matter how hard we tried to go on like nothing had happened.

Then Maile said something that caught me by surprise.

"Kai, I've been with only one other man since Nestor died. The relationship ended when I found out he was seeing someone else." She looked away. "Nobody will ever do that to me again. Even an old friend."

I nodded, having already decided to break it off with Madison. There was no reason Maile would find out about her. And no reason to bring her up now. I don't know much about women, but I do know that a woman expects to be number one in her man's life, with no rival. Introduce a rival, and you introduce trouble. No, I'd remain silent about Madison. Why jinx a promising relationship for one that should have never been?

* * *

By one o'clock nothing had changed at Mrs. Varda's. With barely an hour left before we had to head back, I looked again into her windows. Finally I saw Mrs. Varda herself walking to one of her glass doors. She slid it open. And from a couch, where he had apparently been napping and hidden from our view, Kula ambled behind her onto the pool deck and yawned. The golden retriever's coat lit up in the sun.

"He's *beautiful*." Maile whispered, her eyes glued to him.

The famous surfing dog circled the swimming pool, sniffing the *laua'e* ferns and red ginger on its borders. Mrs. Varda lumbered across the deck and planted her imposing figure in a patio chair.

"What do we do with her?" I asked.

"Got her phone number?"

I nodded.

"I'll call to lure her back into the house. Then we'll take Kula."

Maile flipped open her cell phone.

"Wait," I said. "Shouldn't you take Kula? You're the dog expert. Plus you've got no license to lose if you get caught."

"Kula's met you. He hasn't met me," said Maile. "All you'll need is a plan to get his attention."

"I've got one." I reached into my khakis and pulled out a spanking-new yellow tennis ball.

Maile smiled. "You're a natural, Kai. Now give me her number."

"How will you keep her talking? What if she hangs up?"

"Trust me."

That's why I don't work with a partner. Each of us had a job to do that directly affected the other's and neither of us knew for sure if the other could deliver. I had no choice but to trust Maile would.

She dialed Mrs. Varda's number and took a deep breath. Within seconds we heard the faint ringing of a telephone in the distance. The large woman rose slowly from her deck chair and stepped not into her house, but to a cordless phone on a *lānai* table a few feet away.

"*Oh, sh*—" I said. "She's not going inside. What'll we do now?"

thirty-four

Kula's new mistress picked up her phone.

"Hello, Mrs. Varda?" said Maile. "I'm calling from *Maui Home* magazine. We're planning a special photo feature on Lahaina oceanfront homes next month and we couldn't help noticing that yours is especially charming . . ."

Clever woman.

"Stick to the plan," Maile whispered to me. "This could be our only shot." She signaled to move out.

"Yes, everyone on our staff agrees that your home should be our cover story . . ." she said into her cell phone.

I stepped up to the hedge. *"Kula,"* I called in a whisper. *"Kula, come."*

The golden retriever tilted his head to one side and looked puzzled.

"Kula, come!" I called him again, louder this time.

He trotted toward the gate. Mrs. Varda meanwhile kept talking on her phone, making sweeping gestures, as if giving a grand tour of her home. When Kula reached the gate, he barked.

If his mistress couldn't hear that, she was deaf.

I opened the gate and pulled the tennis ball from my pocket. The retriever stopped barking instantly and stuck his nose so close to the yellow ball I could feel his warm breath on my hand. He eyed it intently. I faced the ocean and cocked my arm. Kula's gaze followed the ball as if he were stalking a yellow bird. He crouched low. His whole body tensed.

When Mrs. Varda looked up from the phone and saw me with her Boomer, her expression changed. She shouted: "Don't let the dog out, please!"

I pitched the ball in one swift arc over the beach, past the shore break, and into the calmer water beyond. Kula bolted across the sand and dove into the surf. He paddled furiously like a blond otter.

Mrs. Varda hung up and hurried to the gate. "Stop!"

I ran down to the water just as Kula caught up with the ball, grasping it in his teeth. Then he turned back to me with a look of pride in his eyes. His birddog genes apparently couldn't care less if it was a yellow bird or yellow ball.

"Kula, come!" I called.

He began paddling back to shore, kicking up a wake behind him. As he stepped dripping onto the sand, Maile appeared with a leather leash and looped it around Kula's neck. "Let's go for a run, boy," she coaxed him, but he'd already started off at a brisk pace.

Mrs. Varda was huffing across the sand now toward us. "Stop! I'll call the police!"

"This is a stolen dog," I shouted to her. "We're returning him to his owner."

"Stolen?" she huffed. "That can't—"

We didn't hear the rest. Maile and I ran up the beach access with Kula in the lead, tennis ball still in his teeth looking like a big goofy yellow smile. I popped open the back hatch of the van and the retriever hopped in. We were his kind of folks, I guess. I jumped behind the wheel, Maile took shotgun, and we squealed away. No Mrs. Varda in the rearview mirror.

"She's probably dialing nine-one-one right now," I said. "We better keep Kula down and out of sight."

Maile climbed into the back and coaxed the soggy dog into the kennel. I aimed the van through Lahaina town and then onto the highway back to Kahului. After all the excitement, Kula lay down inside the crate to rest. Maile stayed with him all the way to the airport, her soothing voice reassuring the dog—and me—that we had done the right thing.

* * *

A few minutes before we pulled into Kahului Airport, my cell phone rang. I made a right turn with one hand, and with the other flipped open the phone, too preoccupied with driving to check caller ID.

"Darling, where are you? I've been calling your apartment and your office all afternoon." *Madison.*

"I'm on a case." I spoke softly. "What's the problem?"

"Conrad's gone back to L.A. I thought you'd want to know."

"So there's no problem?"

"Well, there might be," she replied. "Something strange happened to me today."

"Like what?" I glanced back at Maile. I hoped Madison would be quick.

"I sent a check to Barry Buckingham."

"Really?" Bad idea, I thought. *But it's her money.*

"Then this afternoon driving home from Gucci I tuned in Barry's show, but it wasn't on. The station was playing elevator music."

Uh-oh.

"I started to worry, since I had just sent him a check," Madison went on. "So I called the radio station. The receptionist said the show had been cancelled. She wouldn't say why."

"Hmmm." I couldn't begin to tell her the whole Barry Buckingham story. Not now.

"Then I called Barry's offices and left a message. Well, I left three messages. He hasn't returned any of them."

"When did you mail your check?"

"Saturday."

"Today's Tuesday. It may be too late."

"For what?" Madison sounded worried.

"To put a stop payment on it."

"You think it's that serious?"

"If it is, you'll lose every penny. If it's not, you can always send him another one."

"No wonder Conrad always handles the money," Madison said. "I've made a mess of this!" She hung up, without saying goodbye.

"What was that about?" Maile asked from the back of the van.

"My client's radio program has been yanked off the air. And he's not returning calls."

"What does that mean for Kula?"

"I'm not sure."

thirty-five

At Kahului Airport a skycap helped us load Kula's kennel onto a dolly. Maile stayed with the damp retriever while I returned the van. By the time I made my way to the ticket counter, the two of them were near the front of the line. Inside the kennel Kula hunkered down and glanced at me through the side grates with a bewildered look in his eyes. I felt for him. But I knew we'd have him home in no time.

* * *

It was nearly 5:30 when we claimed Kula at the inter-island terminal in Honolulu. Maile released him in baggage claim and the sunny retriever stepped stiffly from the kennel and then made a beeline for the nearest pillar and lifted his leg.

"Kula!" It was too late.

A yellow stream poured down the pillar and formed a puddle on the tile floor. Maile and I looked at one another. She corralled Kula and slipped on his gold-embossed collar and led him quickly out the door. We walked to the parking garage.

The surfing dog hopped into the back of my Impala where, instead of a seat, my surfboard stretched into the trunk. Kula pressed his nose against the rear window on the driver's side, smeared it, and barked. I cranked down the window. Maile sat in front with me, my board's nose resting on the seat between us. As I pulled from the garage, Kula stuck his head out the window and sniffed the breeze. Maile glanced back at him.

"We should rinse the saltwater off his coat," she said.

"We're going to Wonderview," I said. "Lehua may want to do it herself. She hasn't seen him for a week."

Soon we were climbing Tantalus. Kula grew restless when he saw the familiar winding road. He stuck his head way out the window. His mouth gaped into a big smile. As we pulled up to the white wall surrounding the mansion, Kula's energy rose to a crescendo. He barked and squirmed and tried to jump through the window.

Maile put him on leash and walked him along the white wall where he sniffed and lifted his leg in familiar places. They stopped at the copper gate. Kula barked and Maile attempted to let him in, but the gate was locked. Kula barked again. I tried the gate myself, with no luck. Then I buzzed the intercom.

Silence.

I buzzed again.

I pushed the buzzer one more time and then climbed over the wall. I hiked up the granite steps to the *koa* doors and knocked.

No answer.

I twisted the knob. It wasn't locked. I stepped inside. The entry hall lights were on.

"Hello? Mr. Buckingham? Lehua?" I said.

The only sound was the echoing of my own voice.

I wandered down the hallway. "Mr. Buckingham?"

In a bedroom plastered with surfing posters that I assumed was Lehua's, clothing was scattered on the floor. It looked like the teenager had dressed haphazardly and left in a hurry. I walked to the end of the hallway and opened a door that led to the garage. There sat Lehua's green Mini, but not her father's Rolls. It appeared they were gone.

I walked back into the house. On the opposite side of Lehua's bedroom overlooking the blue sea I found Bucking-ham's office and his master bedroom. The office appeared untouched—except for a wall safe. It was wide open and empty. No cash. No gold. No sign of the pitchman's pistol.

In his mammoth bedroom I found a walk-in closet, bigger than my apartment, that looked like it had been hit by a hurricane. An antique dresser and chest were heaped with clothing and there was another pile on the white carpet. A half-full overnight bag lay next to it. It appeared that Bucking-ham, like his daughter, had grabbed whatever he could carry and ran.

Lying in the open top drawer was a velvet jewelry case. Empty. I slid open the next drawer: Calvin Klein boxers and undershirts. Then the next: button down Oxford shirts in pastel colors. The bottom drawer appeared to be empty. I looked more closely.

Back in a dark corner, where Buckingham had apparently forgotten it, lay a shark's tooth on a broken black cord. Not the sort of jewelry Buckingham wore. I checked out the necklace. The tooth was engraved in scrimshaw with the letter *M*.

Moku Taliaferro.

It could mean only one thing. Buckingham was involved in Moku's murder.

I stuffed the necklace into my pants pocket and called Detective Fernandez, hoping he'd believe me. I got his voice-mail.

"I think I've found the man who crushed Moku's skull, Frank. Barry Buckingham. I'll deliver the evidence to you, but first I'm going after him." I paused and thought. "He probably killed Reiko Infante too. And maybe his own wife. I'm heading down to Ala Moana Yacht Club, where he keeps his boat. It's called the *Golden Hinde*."

Climbing back over the wall I found Maile still walking Kula outside the grounds. The retriever's tail was wagging. He looked happy to be almost home.

"Buckingham left," I said, "in a rush. But he forgot this." I showed her the broken necklace.

"So?"

"It belonged to the man HPD thinks I killed. They say I did it for his necklace. So this could clear me."

Maile glanced at the shark's tooth. "Homicide thinks you killed for this?"

"According to Fernandez."

"He's got to be kidding."

"He's not," I said. "And I don't find it funny."

"Can't say I blame you."

Maile put the reluctant retriever back into the car and I drove down the hill to the yacht club.

* * *

Evening was approaching and Honolulu streets were flowing freely now after rush hour. Within a few minutes we arrived at the harbor.

Kula got antsy again. His tail whacked my surfboard, making the *bop-bop-bop* like a bongo drum. Maile put him back on leash and opened the door. Kula took off like a shot toward the docks.

"Kula, heel!" Maile commanded.

The retriever pulled with purpose. He led us right to the spot where the *Golden Hinde* should have been. That rescue board still was mounted by the empty slip.

But the boat was gone.

thirty-six

Then we saw it. About forty yards from the dock, the big sloop was chugging under diesel power toward the harbor mouth. The gold dealer was at the helm.

"You forgot something, Buckingham," I shouted across the water and dangled Moku's necklace in the air. The shark's tooth glinted in the sun.

Buckingham smiled and waved and said, "Cheers," and kept going. The *Golden Hinde* was headed for the open sea.

Kula was beside himself. His master was leaving him behind. The retriever barked and pulled on his leash.

Maile grabbed the leash with both hands. "Sit!" she said.

The dog kept pulling.

Then from inside the cabin Lehua popped up and saw him on the dock. The girl screamed: *"Kula!"*

Maile tried to hold him back, but when he saw the girl Kula ripped the leash from Maile's hands and dove into the water. He swam toward the sailboat, churning up a white wake behind him. Maile and I watched him from the dock. He was a strong swimmer. And he was moving fast.

"Kula!" Lehua leaned over the sailboat's guardrail.

The dog kept swimming. But he couldn't catch up to the *Golden Hinde*.

The girl turned to her father and we heard her shout: "Daddy, please!"

But Daddy didn't stop, or even slow the boat. Lehua shouted again. Buckingham kept his hand on the throttle. Kula fell farther behind.

Suddenly the girl ran to the stern and jumped overboard.

"Oh, my God!" Maile pointed.

When Buckingham saw his daughter hit the water, he spun the wheel and turned the boat around.

We watched the dog and girl swimming toward each other, and the sloop closing in on them. When I couldn't stand it anymore, I kicked off my sandals, stripped down to my board shorts, and grabbed the rescue board.

I paddled as fast as I could to the middle of the harbor. But Buckingham's boat intercepted Lehua before I could, its starboard bow coming between me and the girl and the dog. Both were on the other side. I couldn't see the two and, luckily Buckingham, who was busy with them, couldn't see me either.

I grabbed onto a vinyl dock bumper hanging from the starboard bow of the *Golden Hinde*. The surfboard had no leash or line to tie to the boat, so I set the board free. Then I pulled myself up on the bumper and strained to see across the deck. Buckingham was bending over the port side, talking with his daughter, who apparently clung onto Kula and to another bumper.

"We'll send for him when we reach Bora Bora," Buckingham was saying.

"I won't go without him," Lehua insisted.

"Get in the boat!" he shouted.

"I don't believe you," she yelled back.

"Lehua!"

Then she said, "C'mon, Kula."

I heard splashes. Next I saw the girl and dog clear the port bow, both of them swimming for the dock. The surfboard I had set free was drifting toward them. Lehua swam for it and climbed on. Then she paddled to Kula and helped him on. The dog crawled to the nose and hung his front paws over the tip, just like I'd seen in the TV news video. The girl paddled for the slip where Maile was waiting.

"Lehua!" Buckingham shouted. "You can bring the dog."

The girl kept paddling.

"Blast you, then!" he screamed across the water. "Blast your mother too! What will you do without me, eh?"

Buckingham returned to the wheel, pushed the throttle forward, and swung the sloop back toward the harbor mouth.

I was dragged through the water as the *Golden Hinde* headed out to sea.

The boat picked up speed. I dropped down on the bumper, keeping my head below deck level. I didn't know what to do. I was unarmed and Buckingham, for sure, would have his snub-nose.

The *Golden Hinde* cleared the harbor jetty and the rock pilings that surround Magic Island—the last spit of land before the open sea. He wasn't turning back. Not even for his own daughter.

Outside the jetty, a summer swell was rolling in. Bowls was ahead off the port side, and it looked six to eight feet, easy. Other breaks were going off. Lots of surfers were carving up the waves. Not me. I was hanging onto that bumper on the starboard side. And if I didn't do something soon, I would be in very deep water.

The *Golden Hinde*'s bow began to rise and fall over the swells. Buckingham shoved the throttle all the way forward and turned *ewa,* or to the west, offshore of Ala Moana Beach. He made no move to raise the sails.

Before long we were making better time than I could ever do on my board. The yacht harbor shrunk behind us in our wake. The boat passed just outside the surf spots off Ala Moana Beach Park: Tennis Courts, Concessions, Big Rights, Marineland, and finally Kewalos. Ahead was Point Panic.

I kept my eye on the gold dealer at the helm. It was time to move.

Another swell rolled under the boat. I hoisted myself up the bumper and rushed across the deck. I took Buckingham down. He went flat on his back. The wheel swung around and the sailboat yawed and started circling. I came down on top of him. He reached into his pocket and showed the snub-nose. I knocked the gun out of his hand. It slid across the deck, coming to rest against a toe rail. The boat kept circling. Going fast, but nowhere.

Buckingham rushed not for the gun, but for the helm. He righted the wheel, punched a button that must have been an autopilot, and the boat stopped going in circles. But now we were headed for Point Panic. The rocks. Full throttle.

The swells started coming at us from behind. The big sloop rode them like a seesaw. The stern rose and then the bow fell. Over and over again. I'm no sailor—I'm a surfer—but it seemed to me that this was no place for a boat to be: its tail to a summer swell and its nose heading for the rocks.

Buckingham came at me on all fours. Before I could get up, he slipped his gold fingers around my neck. Another swell picked us up and the boat rode it like an outrigger canoe. He held onto my throat, trying the strangle the life out of me. I punched him in the ribs. He groaned and loosened his grip. I pushed him off of me and he fell backwards.

Out of the corner of my eye I saw Point Panic. A body surfer was carving a big green barrel. He was milking the wave to the last drop and preparing to bail out before it hit the wall. Then I realized he was parallel to us. The *Golden Hinde* was riding the same wave right next to him! And the rocks were coming.

The wave took us. The boat swept forward in a surge. We were doomed. Buckingham hopped up on the deck and started coming for me again. He would never make it.

"Why'd you kill Moku?" I said as we were about to hit. "He was nobody."

"Hardly, mate." Buckingham kept coming. "He worked for Scan—"

Before he could finish, I heard the crack of the bow hitting the rocks and then a horrible splintering sound. The shock of our impact carried stern-ward. Buckingham, his center of gravity higher than mine, was thrown toward the rocks. The next thing I knew, he was gone and I was in the surf. The *Golden Hinde* lay on its side in splinters next to me.

The swells kept coming. I bobbed among the boat's debris. I tried to swim away from the seawall, but each successive wave washed me closer. In the distance I saw that body surfer who had just milked the same wave swimming toward me. Another wave hit, bringing something heavy and sharp from the wreck with it—more quickly than I could swim.

The lights went out.

thirty-seven

When I opened my eyes I was on a bed inside a pale green room. I felt like I was still floating. Something resembling a clothespin was attached to the tip of my right index finger. My upper left arm was encircled by a python-like band that made a *beep-beep-beep-beep* sound, echoing the beat of my heart. Numbers flashed on a monitor—48—50—52—48—counting the beeps. An IV was stuck in my left arm, connected to a tube and container above the bed. And overhead was the mother of all flood lamps blazing down on me.

I wasn't wearing my board shorts anymore. I was in something resembling a baby-blue nightshirt. Blankets covered me and I was very warm. I raised my left hand and felt my head. It was wrapped in a gauze bandage like a turban. There was a bump on the back of my head, so heavily bandaged I couldn't feel my fingers on my scalp. I lowered my arm and then heard a woman's voice.

"Detective . . ."

Two faces looked down at me. One was unfamiliar—a woman in a smock. The other, I recognized.

"How ya feeling, Kai?" said the homicide detective.

"Frank?"

"Glad you made it," he said.

"Where am I?"

"Queens Hospital. A piece of that wrecked boat smacked you in the head. You damned near drowned. A surfer pulled you out at Point Panic. You've got a pretty nasty gash, but the doc already stitched you up. You should be outta here by tomorrow."

"I don't feel anything," I said.

"You won't," the nurse spoke up, "for a while. But once the anesthetic wears off, you'll be glad for the meds Dr. Masaki prescribed for you."

"I'm not much for drugs." I've always been stubborn about this. I don't like taking anything except vitamins. My parents' New England roots again.

She shook her head, but Fernandez smiled down at me like I was his own son.

"Buckingham?" I wondered aloud about the man who had put me there.

"In surgery," Fernandez said. "Broke his leg and a couple of vertebrae. He's going to be laid up for a while."

"He killed Moku."

"Yeah, I got your message. But when I drove down to the yacht club, it was too late. You were already in the water.

"What about his daughter—

"Don't worry," Fernandez cut me off. "We'll take it from here. Buckingham's not going anywhere. He'll be held on fraud and theft charges, even if we can't hold him yet for murder."

"But what did you do with Lehua?"

"I questioned her. She didn't know much about what her father was into. Then I turned her over to Maile. She's got the dog too." Fernandez ran his fingers through his dark wavy hair. "Maile returned your car, by the way. Nice lady. The K-9 guys all liked her."

I tried to nod, but my head was going nowhere.

A little smile then turned up at the corners of Fernandez's mouth. "So you dating her, or what?"

"She's an old friend. She was helping me with the pet case."

"She hasn't dated much since Nestor died, far as I know. But when she's ready," he adjusted his belt, "yours truly is gonna be first in line."

"Lucky guy," I said.

"You should be so lucky." Fernandez winked and left the room.

* * *

The next afternoon I was released from the hospital. The lump on the back of my head was the size of a block of Sex Wax, the stuff I rub on the deck of my board. But at least I could see straight. And I could walk. I was no longer numb. But I didn't think I would need the painkillers the doc had pre-scribed. Remembering the nurse's warning, I picked them up at the pharmacy anyway, along with an antibiotic and ice pack.

An HPD officer was waiting for me in the lobby when I got out of the elevator. He led me to an unmarked car and we rode to the Beretania Street Station. Fernandez met me in his office and I told him the official version of the Buckingham story. I didn't mention how I bent the law along the way. Frank was supremely satisfied, even without those details.

Finally given a lift to my apartment, I fell into bed and called Maile. After four rings her answering machine kicked in.

"Hi, you've reached Maile Barnes, tracer of missing pets. How can I help?"

"Maile, it's Kai . . ." I waited a few seconds, hoping she would pick up. "I just got out of the—"

"Kai," she said breathlessly, as if she'd run to the phone. "Are you okay? I would've come to the hospital to see you, but I've got Lehua and Kula with me. It's kind of a zoo around here."

"Frank Fernandez told me," I said, glad to hear her voice. "That was good of you to take them both."

"It's just temporary. But they had nowhere else to go. HPD has closed off Buckingham's house. And it's no place for Lehua to be right now anyway—after what's happened."

"How is Lehua?"

"Doing well—considering. She's a nice girl, Kai. I feel sorry for her. I don't think she had any idea what was going on."

"Not until a few days ago," I said. "I think she started to figure out then that her father wasn't the man he pretended to be. It was quite a shock for her. I was there."

"Who's going to take care of her? Her father will be doing time for the rest of his life. And her mother . . ?"

"Her mother's the wild card. If Scanlon didn't kill her or Buckingham himself."

"I hope for Lehua's sake she's alive."

"Me too. But I don't have to tell a veteran cop that after a woman's been missing for months, the odds get very long that she'll be found."

"Speaking of long odds," she said, "how did you survive that ship wreck? Frank said it was miraculous. And how's your head?"

"A surfer pulled me out of the wreckage. I guess I owe him my life.

As for my head, it's just a bump. The doc gave me a few stitches. Nothing serious. I'll be good as new in a few days. Which reminds me, how about that celebration I promised you?"

"I'd love to. When you're feeling better. And when we find out what's going to happen with Lehua and Kula."

"I'll check back." Then I remembered something. "Say, you know Frank Fernandez from Homicide?"

"Sure, everybody at HPD does. Why?"

"Oh, just curious. You know him well?"

"Nestor knew him well. They were buddies. And we used to go out together—Nestor and me, and Frank and his wife. Or should I say ex-wife?"

"I see."

"Oh, you want to know if I ever dated him?"

"Doesn't matter."

"The answer is no. I told you I dated only one person since Nestor died and that ended how I told you it ended."

"None of my business," I said.

"You better get some sleep, brah. Or you're going to have one major headache tomorrow morning."

"The doc gave me pain pills—but I won't need them. I'll be fine."

"Take them, or you'll be sorry."

"Yes, mom."

"Sometimes you may need a mom, Kai. But I'm not her. Just a friend telling you not to be a jerk. Take the pills or you won't sleep a wink."

"Later," I said. "You're the best."

"The feeling's mutual," she said.

I hung up feeling good, never mind the bump on my head.

* * *

After talking with Maile I turned on the TV and stared blankly at a rerun of *Hawaii Five-0*. I didn't feel much from the bump on my head. It didn't hurt, really. And I started thinking I was tough guy. I had survived a shipwreck and a whack on the head. I forgot the nurse's instructions to take the painkillers. Suddenly I was curious to see my wound and figured it was time to change the dressing.

I walked into the closet that passes for a bathroom in my apartment and looked in the mirror. I watched myself peel off the red-soaked gauze and looked in the mirror at the back of my head. The doc had shaved my hair just above the neckline. And there it was—a red, crusty mess, right out of a slasher movie. I was sure it would all look better later, after the swelling and purple went away. But right then it wasn't too pretty. Fresh blood seeped out between the dozen or so stitches. I put on a new bandage, glad to have that mess out of my sight.

I went back and lay in bed. A few minutes passed. Then it started. Around the wound like a mild headache. After a while it turned into a real banger. I put on an ice pack. That helped a little. But not much.

Before long my head was really throbbing. I wasn't such a tough guy after all. I gave in and popped a pain pill. I waited for it to take hold. Meanwhile I tried to fall asleep. But I just lay there, focused on the pain. It felt like somebody was drilling the back of my head. I kept wondering why the pill wasn't working. After fifteen minutes—nothing. I broke down and popped another. More time went by. Finally I started to feel some relief. The throbbing in my head turned down a notch from ten to nine. Then to eight. But by nearly an hour later, the volume was down to only seven . . . maybe.

I wanted the pain to go away. I wanted to sleep. But it wasn't happening. My two painkillers were fighting the doc's dozen stitches. My team was outgunned. So I lay there, waiting for a few more hours to pass so I could pop another pill.

Unable to sleep, I switched the TV to the late news, catching the tail end of the local broadcast.

"And, finally tonight, a mystery at the legendary Royal Hawaiian Hotel in Waikīkī. Hotel security and police are searching for an elderly Australian visitor who disappeared from the famous pink palace two days ago leaving his personal items in his room and an empty leather briefcase with the initials BB on it. Anyone with information about this man, who checked in under the name Abraham Scanlon, should contact the Honolulu Police Department . . ."

It was no mystery to me. One of two things had happened. Either Scanlon had slunk away to parts unknown without paying his hotel bill, or Buckingham got to him first.

thirty-eight

Late the next morning after I managed to drive myself—against doctor's orders—to my office, there was a knock at the door. I opened it to a statuesque Chinese woman in her late forties, in an elegant silk dress.

Next to her was Kula.

The golden retriever looked as surprised to see me as I was to see him. He bounded to my desk, barking and wagging his tail.

"Kula," said the woman. *"Come."*

"He's alright," I said and petted him. "And you are——"

But before I could even finish my sentence, I knew the answer. The exotic elegance, the faint Australian accent, she had to be Cheyenne Sin. So then I said, "You're Barry Buckingham's wife."

"Soon to be ex-wife." She glided into the office, her dress clinging to every hill and valley of her picturesque terrain. A few years earlier and she could have stepped off the pages of *Glamour.*

As she sat in my client's chair, I settled behind my desk and Kula followed me. He sat and I stroked his soft fur.

"I'm taking Lehua away from here, Mr. Cooke. I can't say where, but I'm sure you understand why." She spoke as elegantly as she dressed. "The recriminations against Barry are going to rebound on us. There will be no place safe in Hawai'i for Lehua and me. Not only that, Barry could drag me into his troubles and our daughter might end up with neither parent to care for her."

I patted the dog and nodded. "How did you find her at Maile's?"

"I called Lehua's cell phone when I heard of Barry's arrest. I picked her up—and Kula—this morning." She rolled on. "Lehua can't part with him, of course. But we leave tonight and we simply don't have time to get him the necessary inoculations and documentation. He's got to remain in Hawai'i until those things can be obtained."

"I see," I said, wondering what all this had to do with me.

"Lehua trusts you, Mr. Cooke. She trusts you so much, she's going to leave her dog with you."

"But . . ."

"Just temporarily. And if you wouldn't mind taking him surfing now and then, he'd be in seventh heaven."

My face must have registered my astonishment.

"Of course, we're going to compensate you," she quickly added. She took an envelope from her purse and dropped it on my desk. "One thousand dollars—in cash. For your trouble and for Kula's upkeep until he joins us."

"Wait a minute," I stopped her. I needed to make sense of the strange direction the case was taking—and had come from. "Have you been hiding this whole time?"

"Yes, from Barry . . . Well, from Abe too."

"Hiding from both of them?"

"Yes. I never divorced Abe. When he found me in Honolulu, he threatened to kill me. At the time, Barry was blaming me for all our money troubles." She sighed. "Our fights escalated to the point that I decided to disappear. But I couldn't be far from Lehua."

"Mrs. Gum . . ."

"Yes, Mrs. Gum was kind enough to take me in, even making up that story about Barry feeding me to the sharks. I thought he had hired you to find me."

"And you're who I saw in the upstairs window?"

Cheyenne Sin nodded. "Sometimes I snuck out at night and peeked into my daughter's bedroom window to reassure myself she was alright. I felt so terrible, watching her cry over my being gone. But I started fearing for my own life and just bolted. I tried to get a message to her, without her father knowing. I almost got caught, though. I even once set off the alarms."

"So you were the prowler your husband thought was casing his property?"

She nodded again. "When we first met in Sydney, Barry was solicitous of my every need. But as time wore on, he changed. You know what they say—all that glitters isn't gold."

I leaned farther back in my chair. Kula had found a comfortable position resting against my leg, his head in my lap. "Well, I appreciate the trust you and Lehua have put in me," I said, "and I appreciate the money, but I can't—"

"We know you'll take good care of Kula." Cheyenne Sin stood and headed for the door. "We'll be in touch."

Kula watched his mistress leave. To my surprise, he didn't move a muscle. I patted him again, but he needed no reassurance.

* * *

Within minutes I had loaded the golden retriever into my Impala and was driving to Mānoa. I didn't call first. I didn't even consider how Maile would respond to see Kula again so soon.

I knocked on the door of her cottage and she came in shorts and a t-shirt, her brown hair down. Maile looked at Kula and me standing there. Before she could get a word out, the three cats scattered.

"Coconut! Peppah! Lolo!" she shouted after their disappearing tails. "You remember Kula." Then to me: "I don't know what's wrong with them. They got on well with him before. C'mon in."

"I'm sure they'll get used to him again," I said as I walked inside, the dog leading the way. "At least I hope they will."

"So how are you, Kai?" Maile looked me up and down. "How's your head?"

"Okay."

"Let me see." She put her hand on my shoulder, looked at the bandage on the back of my head, and then kissed me.

"I feel much better now," I said, whiffing her loamy fragrance.

"And your stitches?"

"All good . . ." I said as I wondered how to approach her about Kula.

"Is there something you want to tell me?"

"Tell you?"

"Well, here you are unannounced with this beautiful animal . . . I was just wondering what's going on."

"The strangest thing happened today," I said as we sat down. "You wouldn't believe. Well, I wouldn't have believed it if it hadn't happened in my office." I paused. "You met Buckingham's wife this morning?"

"Yes, go on . . ."

So I told her about Cheyenne Sin showing up with Kula and telling me the story she did and then leaving him behind with me. I went into detail. Maile latched onto every word, as if the story involved her own best friend. I worked up slowly to the point, trying to come up with a graceful lead-in to the huge favor I was about to ask. But there was no way to soft peddle it. So I just popped the question.

"Maile, would you mind keeping Kula for a few days?" I had no idea how many, but days sounded better than weeks or months. "I'd take him myself, but I've got nowhere to keep him."

"Me? Take Kula?" Maile looked slightly bewildered. She bent down and ran her fingers through his golden fur. She didn't say anything for a while. Then softly: "No, I don't mind . . ."

"Are you sure?" I said. It wasn't like Maile to be any way but direct. She usually said what was on her mind—like when she told me not to be a jerk about taking my painkillers.

"It's fine, really." Kula's tail was waving like a victory flag. "I just haven't had a dog in the house since Rusty—"

"Thanks," I said, relieved. "Thanks a lot."

She crouched down and put her arms around the dog. I thought I saw tears in her eyes. She buried her face in his fur.

Kula had found himself a new home. At least for now.

In a minute Maile looked up. Her face was streamed with tears. I didn't know what to say. I handed her two of the hundreds Cheyenne Sin had given me. Maile shook her head, as if to say it wasn't necessary.

"There's more where that came from." I walked silently to the door and let myself out. Seemed to me, she and the dog needed to be alone.

thirty-nine

Wednesday's *Star-Advertiser* detailed the wreck of the *Golden Hinde*, with photos of the capsized boat in shallow water off Point Panic. There was also a file photo of me, and one of Buckingham in his three-piece suit. Buckingham was the prime suspect in the murders of Moku Taliaferro and Reiko Infante, not to mention multiple counts of fraud and theft and tax evasion. The story said his radio program had been cancelled. Buckingham owed Honolulu station KGHO an unspecified sum for unpaid air time. Two investors were interviewed who had purchased gold from Buckingham and received worthless certificates in return. He claimed he held the gold in his personal vaults, saving clients the expense of secure storage. But he never made good on his claim.

The story did not make a connection between Buckingham and the disappearance of Abe Scanlon from the Royal Hawaiian Hotel. Whether Buckingham had killed the old Aussie or he was wandering loose on the island, I would have liked to know. Also the whereabouts of his lieutenant, Spyder Silva. I don't take threats lightly.

* * *

In the next morning's mail I received a check from High-camp Hotels and Resorts corporate headquarters in Los Angeles. Twenty-five hundred dollars for "services rendered to Mrs. Highcamp." There was no note. Subtracting about five hundred for unrecovered expenses from the Buckingham case, I was now two grand ahead. I didn't count the one thousand from Cheyenne Sin for Kula's care, since Maile already had two hundred of it. And I would no doubt be giving her more.

I saw Maile later that afternoon. Kula was lounging on her rattan sofa like a crown prince. He didn't even bother to bark when he saw me. He just waved his tail. An assortment of raw-hide chews, three new tennis balls, and a braided tug rope were scattered about the room. Peppah and Coconut sat on nearby chairs, keeping their envious eyes on the returned prince.

"Kula isn't putting you out, is he?" I asked Maile.

"He's no bother," she said nonchalantly. "I don't mind him hanging around . . ." She paused and thought for a moment. "When do you think they'll want him back?"

"I haven't heard a word from Lehua or her mother," I said. "But Kula couldn't have found a better home."

I suddenly felt a stab of guilt. The haunting eyes and skeletal forms of Sammy Bob Picket's captives contrasted starkly to the comfort and pampering Kula was enjoying. "Remember that Big Island hoarder I told you about," I said, "the one who sold Kula to the woman on Maui?"

Maile nodded.

"We should turn him in."

"Trouble is," she said, "any seized animals that are sick or can't be adopted might be euthanized."

"Not good."

"I'm sure the Humane Society would do everything it could to place the dogs. I mean the only other way is kind of radical."

"How radical?" I asked.

"We could free the dogs ourselves and place them in a private animal sanctuary."

"We did manage to get Kula out," I said, but I wasn't sure I wanted to try again with dozens of dogs.

"I don't think there are any suitable sanctuaries on the Big Island," she said. "But I can find out."

We left it at that.

* * *

Heading back out of the Mānoa valley, I remembered puppy mill Lou, whose animal abuse was nearly as horrific as Picket's. But she was small time and here on Oʻahu. Through Maile's local contacts, I didn't doubt we could take Lou down once we returned from the Big Island.

I'd barely gotten to the valley's mouth when my phone rang.

"We can go tomorrow," Maile said.

"Go where?"

"To the Big Island. I called Utah after you left and explained the situation. Turns out, some people there know of a woman who's starting up a 'no kill' shelter near Hilo. She's an ex-ALF member."

"Ex-what?"

"ALF—Animal Liberation Front. You know, the ones who wear ski masks and break into labs that experiment on animals. Their detractors call them terrorists."

"I've heard of ALF, but not around here."

"Her name is Deirdre. She's Canadian," Maile continued. "We can stop by and see her shelter tomorrow, then check out your hoarder."

"You don't mind? You don't have a case?"

"Not at the moment," she said.

"OK, but we better go to Sammy Bob's place after dark. If he knows Kula was stolen from Maui, he also knows who did it."

forty

The next afternoon, a Friday, I arrived at the Waikīkī Canoe Club for lunch with a potential client. I wore my best aloha shirt—it was Rayon but looked like silk—and my newest khakis that still had a crease in the legs. I had reserved a 3:05 p.m. flight to Hilo for Maile and me. We planned to drop by the ex-ALF's animal sanctuary, then drive up to Laupāhoehoe in the evening and case Picket's canine prison after dark.

My potential client, a pale and balding accountant named Martin Fix, was looking for someone to investigate his young second wife. Mr. Fix wanted evidence of her infidelity, photos of the Mrs. in bed with the other man. Not my favorite kind of case. But it was all I had going at the moment. And I wasn't taking any more cases involving pets, despite phone messages daily offering me work in that line.

I explained to Mr. Fix that Hawai'i is a no-fault divorce state. Photos of his wife would not be admissible in court, nor would they be necessary. He didn't care. He intended to confront her with the evidence, for whatever reason.

As the soft-spoken Mr. Fix told me his tale of woe, I couldn't help noticing the contrast between his frail arms and those of a tanned and brawny canoe club paddler sitting nearby. Mr. Fix appeared to be a nice and decent man. But apparently being nice and decent hadn't kept his wife from straying. The more I listened to him, the more I could imagine the shoals upon which his marriage had foundered. I knew this pattern all too well: Younger woman. Older man. A third party. Just fill in the blanks.

During lunch, out of the corner of my eye, I spotted Madison Highcamp at an oceanfront table with her usual martini, cigarette, and cell phone. She was alone—except for Twinkie. I hadn't talked to Madison since her frantic call about the gold dealer. It had been a few days. Not hearing from her made me wonder if she was turning over a new leaf after her husband's surprise visit.

Mr. Fix saw her and raised his brows. "If my wife's affairs were as notorious as that Highcamp woman's, I wouldn't need to hire you."

Madison noticed me just then. She made a little come hither gesture with her head.

"Excuse me," I said to Mr. Fix. "Her husband"—I pointed to Madison—"is a client of mine."

"Conrad Highcamp?" he said, sounding impressed, "The hotel tycoon?"

"Afraid so," I replied.

Madison stood when I approached and kissed my cheek. "Where have you been, darling?" She then retrieved Twinkie, who was already climbing my leg.

"I've been on a case," I said, wondering how she could have missed the news stories that would have answered her question. "Anyway, you were with your husband."

"That was days ago." She sounded miffed.

"He paid me, you know." I tried to change the subject. "I got a check in the mail."

"Conrad told me," she said. "And I stopped my check to Barry Buckingham. My money is safe."

"I'm glad." I didn't bother to tell her the gold dealer was at Queens Hospital under guard.

"I like the way you look out for me, Kai." She smiled. "Thank you, darling."

I stood there awkwardly as Mr. Fix gawked at us. "Listen, Madison, I've got a new client over there and I can't afford to keep him waiting."

"Call me, Kai. I have something to tell you. After Conrad left I thought about what you said. I've made a decision."

That worried me. I'd said a lot of foolish things when we were together, most of them forgettable.

"You know Mrs. Highcamp well?" Mr. Fix asked when I returned. "Though I guess all those wealthy society women kiss when they greet you, don't they?"

"Mrs. Highcamp is out of my league," I said casually.

"It's probably better that way," he said. "The stories I've heard . . ."

forty-one

When I picked up Maile for our flight to Hilo, she carried a duffle filled with the tools of her trade. But I wasn't prepared for the rifle case tucked under her arm.

"You're bringing your Remington?"

"Picket pointed a shotgun at you, Kai."

"Look. If it would make you feel better, I can pack my Smith & Wesson," I said. "And I'll deal with the red tape at check in."

Maile gave me stink-eye. "Kai, in fifteen years on the force I qualified with a half dozen firearms and I medaled with this one. We are going up against an armed criminal. I've seen what they can do. It's too close to home."

"OK, Maile, bring your rifle." I relented.

She walked past me to my car.

* * *

At the Honolulu Airport Maile filled out the appropriate forms and checked through her Remington, scope, and ammo. By four that afternoon we landed in Hilo and were driving north in a white van to the coastal town of Pāpaʻikou. We turned *mauka* on a narrow strip called Ka'ie'ie Homestead Road and drove for what seemed like miles. The road rose slowly into the foothills of Mauna Kea. Soon the pavement ended.

"What do we do now?" I said.

Maile glanced at her handwritten directions. "Keep going on this dirt road."

It was just a Jeep path, really, that zigzagged through hills and woods, reminding me of Picket's haunt. Finally we reached a dry creek bed and the road ran out.

"This must be it," Maile said.

"What? There's nothing here."

But I was wrong. A small cottage, that could barely be seen, stood in the distance with a rusting VW Golf parked out front. As we hiked toward the cottage, Maile explained that Deirdre was just getting started with her animal shelter. The sun was still overhead and it was hot. Very hot. After only a few steps I could feel sweat forming on my forehead.

A tall, very thin woman opened the door of the cottage and walked toward us. She was a vegan, according to Maile. I guess that accounted for her thinness. She had long silver-flecked black hair that reminded me of sixties folk singer, Joan Baez. I expected Deirdre to launch into "The Night They Drove Old Dixie Down."

"Deirdre Osteen." She reached out her hand. "And you must be Maile? And Kai?"

"Thanks for helping us on such short notice." Maile shook her hand. Then it was my turn. The hand was graceful and lean, like the rest of her. And warm.

"Anything I can do," Deirdre said. "As you can see, I'm just getting started here. I had to leave LA in kind of a hurry."

"You mentioned that on the phone," Maile said. "But Kai hasn't heard the story."

"I'll tell you about it . . ." Deirdre said "about" with the long "o" of Canadian English. "But first, come on inside and get out of the sun."

We walked with her to the cottage. The rusty Golf was parked by the door and my eye caught its bumper sticker: BIO-DIESEL: NO WARS NEEDED. Deirdre must have seen me gawking at it.

"The Golf is a TDI," she said. "It runs on one-hundred percent recycled vegetable oil. The fuel is made right here in Hawai'i."

"Your car is a vegan," I said, "just like you." I meant it to be funny, but she didn't take it that way.

"The big oil companies are almost as bad as animal abusers. They've fought saving the planet every step of the way, and they're scheming to run the bio-fuel industry out of business."

"Not if you can help it." I thought about the gas-guzzling V8 in my old Impala and wondered if I should turn over a new leaf.

Inside the place was basically one room and looked more like a camp than a home. The windows were open and a little breeze flowed through. There were a few cots and some beach chairs and a folding table. The only lamps I could see were battery powered, but not turned on at this time of day. From the personal gear piled in corners of the room, it looked like Deirdre might have a companion, but he or she wasn't around at the moment. And she didn't mention that anyone else was living there. We pulled three chairs into a small circle and sat.

"Jasmine tea?" Deirdre asked. "It's herbal. No caffeine."

Maile accepted and I passed. Deirdre went for a jar with a brownish liquid inside and several teabags. She poured glasses for Maile and herself and returned.

"It's sun tea. The electricity isn't hooked up yet," Deirdre said. "So I serve it at room temperature. I'm kind of keeping a low profile for now."

"Tell Kai what happened," Maile said and sipped her tea.

Maile had already told me that Deirdre Osteen was an animal rights activist from Ontario, Canada, who had spent the last few years in Los Angeles, heavily involved with ALF. But what Mailed didn't say, and Deirdre now did, was that she had been with a cell of ski-masked comrades that ransacked a university research lab and released dozens of caged monkeys, then spray-painted "Meat is Murder" on every available surface at four fast-food restaurants, and finally were about to hit a high-end furrier on Rodeo Drive when three of her comrades got nabbed.

"Before the day was out," Deirdre said with that long "o" again, "I was on a plane to Kona. I have some friends there and I stayed with them while I looked for land to set up a sanctuary. I decided my days with ALF were over. I'm committed to animal rights but I can't be effective if I'm in jail. So I hit on this idea. A no-kill shelter."

"How much land do you have here?" I asked.

"About twenty acres," she said. "I got a good deal on it. It's far from any town or village, as you saw, and access to the property isn't exactly, well, a super-highway."

I wondered how she could afford to buy so much land on the Big Island, but didn't ask. From her nonchalance and quiet confidence she struck me as a child of privilege.

"You're out in the middle of nowhere," Maile said.

"That's perfect for the shelter," Deirdre replied. "No one around to complain about animal smells and noises. Plus I'm starting a garden out back. By the way, do you want something to eat? I'm afraid I don't have much in the way of meat or dairy, but lots of raw vegetables and tofu."

"I'm good," I said, wishing I could sink my teeth into a cheeseburger.

Maile nodded in agreement.

"Well, about your mission," Deirdre said. "I've heard rumors about the man you're going to see."

"Sammy Bob Picket," I said. "We're not going to see him. I've done that already. Once is enough. He's got a shotgun and likes to wave it around."

"We're going to case his property," Maile said. "See his animals and how he keeps them . . . or how he abuses them."

"I've heard he's unstable and prone to violence," Deirdre added. "And like I told you, Maile, I'm willing to take his animals. I'll do the best I can with what I have so far, which isn't much."

"They'll be ten times better off," Maile replied.

"I wish I could help you rescue them," Deirdre said. "I'm sorry. My heart is with you, but I can't run this shelter from jail. I need to lie low for a while."

We declined her offer of ski masks, but listened to everything she could tell us about raiding a facility. When she walked us back to the van she spotted Maile's rifle through the window.

"ALF is a nonviolent organization," she said. "They might break the law when they liberate animals, but they don't condone firearms. I've left the organization, but I still feel that way."

"The rifle is just a precaution. We're dealing with an armed and dangerous man," Maile said. "Tonight we're just going to survey the site and figure out the best way to free his dogs. But if he pulls his shotgun, we will protect ourselves."

* * *

It was twilight by the time I drove the white van into Laupāhoehoe. In growing darkness, I turned onto the dirt road I had taken before to the shadowy undergrowth of Picket's hideout. As I parked, Maile grabbed her Remington.

"Do we really need that just to look around?"

Maile put her hands on her hips. "OK. Between you and Deirdre, I'm outnumbered. But if anything happens, it's your *'ōkole*."

"My *'ōkole* will be just fine," I said.

As Maile put the gun back into the van I had second thoughts. No doubt that Pickett was dangerous. And pet theft, even for a good cause, was still theft. We were already guilty on one count.

In the moments before complete darkness we hiked into the jungle that surrounded Picket's shack. It wasn't long before we heard the faint mournful moans and whiffed the stink.

Rounding a bend, we could clearly see the place. It was dark inside, but a naked bulb on a pole outside cast a harsh glare. I pointed out the fire pit in front where, on my earlier visit, I had seen charred dog collars and blackened tags and licenses. The absence of light inside suggested that either Sammy Bob wasn't at home or had turned in early. Or maybe just passed out drunk.

In the clearing beyond fire ring, at the edges of light, we glimpsed the dark shapes of dozens of dogs, still chained to rusting vehicles and cast-off appliances, or cobbed-together wood crates. Nearer to the shack his two pit bulls slept, well illuminated and secured by their thick leather leads. I hoped they slept soundly.

Gazing upon this dismal scene, Maile's expression registered something between disgust and awe.

"I've seen enough here," she said matter-of-factly. "Let's hike the perimeter and survey the site from other angles."

We kept our distance as we hiked so the dogs wouldn't see or smell us. Maile stopped every so often studying each new angle of that dog ghetto. When we returned to the fire pit, Picket's hovel was still unlit.

Maile tiptoed into the center of the ring and scanned the charred collars and tags. She looked around until she found something that interested her, then reached down and picked up a metal fragment. She held it in front of her for a long time, tilting it this way and that in the harsh light, focusing intently.

Suddenly her head bowed, as if she were praying. She shoved the blackened memento into one of her pockets and stepped abruptly away from the fire pit. She marched past me, her eyes glistening.

"What's wrong?" I asked as she headed in the direction of the van.

"I'll be right back." She disappeared into the darkness.

forty-two

I walked toward the fire ring to check it out myself, stepping over and around the charred logs scattered on its boundary. I should have known better. In the darkness my foot caught one of the logs. I went down. I hit the ground with a thud hard enough to knock the wind out of me and make the stitches in the back of my head throb. And loud enough to wake the pit bulls.

Uh-oh. They growled and pulled against their leather straps. From my position flat on my face in the dirt I looked up and saw right into their empty yellow eyes. One by one, other dogs woke up and started barking.

A light went on inside Picket's shack. The door banged open. He stumbled out bare-chested, his flabby gut hanging over a pair of jeans half tucked into hunting boots. A shotgun trembled in his hands.

"Whut 'n hell yah do'n ta mah dogs? Ah gonna shoot yo' ass!"

I was too close to him to run.

Sammy Bob Picket peered down at me with bloodshot eyes. A surprised look came over his face.

"Geeooorge?" His surprise turned to anger. "Yah sonofabitch! Yah stole that dog on Maui. Didn't ya? Stole 'em an' got me in trouble with the lady. An' yah nevah paid me that other hundret, either."

"You stole the dog." I caught my breath and slowly got up.

"Ah didn't steal 'em. Ah only give 'em a good home. A fellah named Spyder done brought me that dog. But Ah 'spect yah know that. Ah 'spect yah kilt his lady friend. An' now yah come tah git me." He leveled his shotgun.

"I didn't kill anybody."

"Prepare to meet yo' maker, boy."

Picket cocked his shotgun with a metallic click. There was no sense in running. I stood my ground. I had been hit only once in my life—a small-caliber pistol, that left a superficial wound. A shotgun would be different. Especially at close range. I braced.

Then I heard a second metallic click in the distance, and four loud pops.

But the blows never came.

The pit bulls were loose and sprinting toward me! I suddenly feared a death worse than by shotgun. But the dogs darted past me and went for Picket. He turned back to his shack, as his shotgun fell in front of him and landed in the red dirt.

Boom!

The load with my name on it went up into thin air. Sammy Bob swung open the door and tried frantically to pull it closed behind him. But he was too late. One pit bull clamped onto the boot of his trailing leg. The other did the same. It was a strange, savage scene as the pit bulls ripped and tore at the boot still attached to Picket's foot.

Soon Maile was standing over me with her Remington, smelling of gunpowder.

"C'mon, Kai," she said. "Help me save this scum."

"What?"

Maile pulled a small aerosol canister from her pants pocket.

"Pepper spray?" I asked.

She nodded. "Under the circumstances it's the most humane way." She handed the Remington to me and approached the two dogs. "Aim my rifle at the dogs. If one attacks me, you know what to do."

I pointed in the direction of the crazed pair.

"On my count," she said. Then "One—Two—Three!" Maile leaped in front of the dogs and sprayed the aerosol in their faces. The blasts were short, but the results were instantaneous. Both dogs began flailing about blindly, coughing and gasping for air.

"It'll wear off." Maile said as she stepped back. "I'll tie them up again before it does."

"And I'll tie up Picket."

"Take this." She handed me the pepper spay.

I took it in my left hand but kept her rifle in my right. I stepped inside the shack, where Picket was sprawled on the filthy floor, groaning. I could hear whines and barking coming from the closet-sized rooms. I glanced down at the man responsible and wondered why he wasn't dead.

"Mah leg," Sammy Bob moaned and looked up at me blurry-eyed. "Ah can't walk."

He had removed his boot and pulled up his pant leg. There was torn flesh and blood on his lower calf. He also had dark purple bruises around his ankle and foot. But he wasn't going to die.

"Yah gonna he'p me, Georgie boy?" he asked in a suddenly kind, slurred voice. He wasn't just sleepy and hurt, he was also drunk. He seemed to think I'd returned to being his buddy.

I looked around his shack for something to tie him up with. A half dozen chewed-up leashes were lying in a corner by the door. I grabbed two and rolled Picket over on his stomach. I didn't need the pepper spray. There wasn't any fight left in him. I bound his feet, wrapping a towel around his injured ankle. Then I tied his hands behind his back. I didn't bother to gag him. There was no one out there to hear him.

"Yah jus' gonna leave me like this? Ah thought yah wuz my frien'."

"I'll send for help," I said and closed the door behind me. *But I won't rush to do it,* I added to myself.

Across from the shack, Maile had finished securing the pit bulls. As I walked over, I noticed that their eyes were still dilated and their breathing hoarse.

"How'd they get loose?"

"You told me the dogs hated Picket, so I aimed for their leads. It took me four shots and some luck."

"Why didn't you just shoot him? He almost killed me."

"He needs to be held accountable for what he's done."

I handed her Remington back to her.

"You shouldn't second-guess me, Kai," she said. "Or maybe next time it *will* be your *'ōkole*."

forty-three

Deirdre arrived later that night in her biodiesel Golf and, despite her earlier doubts, helped us rescue the dogs. Only afterward did we alert Big Island Police to Picket's whereabouts. We left the pit bulls and three other dogs we found dead, as evidence of his cruelty. It would be obvious to police that many more animals had been held captive there, though we felt sure Picket wouldn't admit it.

The next morning on the plane back to Oʻahu, Maile took out the charred metal piece she had found in the fire pit. She held it in the sunlight streaming through the airplane's window.

It was a pet ID tag. Just a fragment, but the name was clear: *Rusty.*

Maile had spared Sammy Bob Picket—the man who had caused her so much pain—to bring him to justice. Once a good cop, always a good cop.

* * *

I spent Saturday morning in my office, catching up on paperwork and reading the *Star-Advertiser*. It had another story about Buckingham. And I also saw this:

> ### Mililani Puppy Mill Raided
>
> Police stormed a townhouse yesterday in Mililani and found 14 malnourished adult golden retrievers and nearly two dozen puppies. The dogs had been kept in unsanitary conditions for many months, said Hawaiian Humane Society spokesperson, Megan Watanabe. The owner of the property, Louise M. Donner, known to neighbors as "Lou," has been charged with thirty-seven counts of animal cruelty. Neighbors were alerted to problems at the townhouse by what was described as an "awful" smell coming from the home, "as if something had crawled inside and died." But it was pet detective Maile Barnes and private investigator Kai Cooke who first discovered the maltreated animals when working on another case. The rescued dogs were taken to the Hawaiian Human Society on King Street. Most have been turned over for foster care to the Golden Retriever Club of Hawai'i in private homes . . .

I wished the paper hadn't mentioned Maile or me. If Scanlon were still alive, he didn't need any help linking the two of us. We were the pair that had derailed his blackmail scheme. Before I could dwell much on that, there was a knock at my door. I set aside the paper and went for the knob.

In stepped Madison Highcamp in a low-cut leopard print dress that showed more of her than anybody on the street ought to have the right to see. Her red hair hung down to her shoulders like a sheet of fire. Gone was her usual cigarette. And her cell phone. And her Maltese. But her intoxicating scent of Chanel clung to every part of her.

"Madison, what are you doing in Chinatown?" She'd never come to my office before.

"So this is where you work, darling?" She kissed me full on the lips, and then gazed from my desk, in its normal disarray, to my only window overlooking Maunakea Street. "It's . . . *quaint.*"

"Never thought of it that way." I pointed her to my client's chair. As she sat down the bounce of her barely concealed breasts hit my nerve ends like a thunderbolt.

"Kai, you didn't call me."

"I've been on a case, Madison. I got back late last night. What's up?"

"Us."

"Us?" I said. "You and me?"

She nodded. "I told you I'd been thinking about what you said. Well, I've made a decision."

"What did I say?"

"You said, 'Have you ever thought of divorce?'"

"Have you?" I was stalling.

"After Conrad left I thought about it a lot." She sat up straight. "I'm going to be brave, Kai. I'm going to file the papers."

"But you'll get nothing. You said so yourself."

"That's true. I will get nothing. I don't care. Some things are more important than money." She caressed her long hair and looked into my eyes. "Aren't they, Kai?"

"Madison, you may think you don't need money, but you've never lived without it." That might have been a cruel thing to say at that moment, but it was the truth.

"You're afraid of commitment," she shot back. "You want me when it suits you, but otherwise you never call." She fumbled nervously with her Gucci handbag, her fingers digging inside the saddle leather.

"You can't smoke here."

"Damn!" She slammed down her bag. "I'm trying to quit. But I need one right now."

"I haven't got any, Madison."

She searched my eyes.

"Hey, where's your faithful companion?" I tried to change the subject. "You don't go anywhere without Twinkie."

"She's at the doggie boutique getting groomed," Madison said, softening. "That girl's hair is more expensive than mine. Oh, that reminds me . . ." Her mood lightened. "Twinkie's groomer said one of her clients lost her Lhasa Apso. I told her you found that missing surfing dog. Her client is desperate."

"No more pet cases," I said. "But I know someone else." From my top desk drawer I pulled one of Maile's cards and handed it to her. "She can give it to her client."

Madison scanned the card. "Is she good?"

"She is," I said, "She helped me rescue Kula."

"She went with you to Maui? And the Big Island?"

I nodded.

"Just the two of you?" Madison sounded suspicious. I was starting to regret giving her Maile's card.

"It was a case, Madison." Luckily the phone rang just then. I picked up on the first ring.

"Hey, Kai, did you hear the one—"

"Hang on a minute, Tommy?" I said into the phone. I turned to Madison. "It's my attorney. This may take awhile."

She frowned and started for the door. "Call me tonight."

"OK."

forty-four

I didn't call Madison that night. And she didn't call me.

A few mornings later, and more than two weeks after Barry Buckingham had first hired me, I was sitting in my office scanning the *Star-Advertiser* when I saw this:

Gold Dealer Indicted for Murder, Fraud

Radio pitchman Barry Buckingham, recuperating at Queen's Hospital from injuries suffered when his yacht, *Golden Hinde,* ran aground at Point Panic near Kewalo Basin last Tuesday, has been indicted on two counts of murder in the first degree and multiple counts of fraud. H.P.D. Homicide Detective Frank Fernandez announced at a news conference yesterday that Buckingham has been charged in the murders of Waimanalo resident Moku Taliaferro and Reiko Infante of Kailua.

> Buckingham made a name and fortune for himself as the charismatic host of "The Gold Standard" daily radio program on KGHO, where he pitched and sold precious metals. Several former clients have filed lawsuits against him. Attorney Michael R. Holstein, who represents one of those clients, told the *Star-Advertiser:* "Barry Buckingham is a classic con man. Court records will show that he has defrauded island residents out of millions of dollars . . ."

The case of Barry Buckingham—my first and only pet case—was officially closed. The story made no mention of Abe Scanlon or his sidekick Spyder Silva. If Buckingham hadn't managed to kill both before his arrest, I hoped Scanlon and Silva would be laying low. I didn't want trouble from either of them.

* * *

A few nights later I had a date with Maile at Ah Fook in Chinatown to celebrate wrapping up the case. We planned to meet at six. I arrived fifteen minutes early. There wasn't much of a crowd at that hour, so I waited outside alone on River Street.

At 6:00, a few customers wandered up and went inside. By 6:15, she still hadn't shown. Patrons were filling the tables inside, so I left my name with the hostess. It didn't seem like Maile to be late.

When 6:30 came and went, I called her cell phone. "Hi, you've reached Maile Barnes, tracer of missing pets. How can I help?"

"Maile, it's Kai. I'm at the restaurant. Are you OK? Call me on my cell."

I called her home phone too, but she didn't answer there either. I left the same message.

I waited until 7:00, then I called both numbers again. Still no response. I was worried. I left Ah Fook without eating and drove up to Mānoa.

On the way I got a sinking feeling, pulled over, and called Madison.

"Helloooo," Madison slurred. She'd evidently had a few martinis at the club.

"Madison, it's me. Did you call Maile Barnes?"

"Yooo gave me her card, darling."

"What did you tell her?"

Silence.

"What did you say?"

"I tol' her the truth, honey, that we're talking about getting married."

I was speechless.

"Kai?"

I hung up.

By then it was dark. And I was disoriented. Instinctively I punched in Maile's number. Of course she didn't answer. I left a message:

"Maile, it's me . . ." I started rambling. "Madison lied. We're not getting married. We're not even dating. I stopped seeing her after I met you—" I could have gone on, but what was the use? Maile wasn't going to answer.

I drove to her cottage thinking I'd just blown it with the girl of my dreams. Never mind that Madison had lied. Never mind that it wasn't really my fault.

The damage had been done.

forty-five

Driving into Mānoa I recalled when I first saw Maile again after so many years. She was in her jogging togs and her face was flushed. She looked terrific. But I was too hung up on Madison at the time to really see Maile. When I told her the last man I interviewed for the case died, she didn't even ask about Dr. Carreras. But that was her way. Take things in stride—like a good cop.

When I pulled up to her cottage a few lights were on. Maile's car was parked out front, so I naturally assumed she was home. I walked to the door and knocked. No answer.

I wasn't surprised. If Maile thought I betrayed her, why would she come to the door?

I knocked again.

Then I tried the knob.

Unlocked. I walked into the familiar room—comfortable and easy-going and island-style like Maile herself. Open jalousies admitted a balmy breeze. Rattan furniture sat on Oriental rugs. But the three cozy cats that usually warmed the cushions were in hiding. Maybe Peppah and Coconut had taken after Lolo? The two gregarious cats weren't afraid of me, and by now should have been nuzzling me and climbing my pant leg. I expected a cool greeting from their mistress, but not the cold shoulder from them. And where was Kula?

"Maile?" I said.

No reply.

I looked around. Kula's water and food dishes, bearing his name in fancy gold lettering, sat on the kitchen floor. Both were full with drink and kibble. By the dishes lay a yellow tennis ball, bringing back memories of Maui. In the kitchen I saw Peppah hiding under the dining table. That wasn't like him. He made eye contact with me, but didn't dash in my direction. He didn't even move. What's going on here? The cats seemed to be sensing something was wrong.

I turned from the Angora and scanned Maile's photo collection—snapshots of her past life. Her husband Nestor in police blues, Maile herself with her rifle, and her dog Rusty— missing and never found. During the course of our investigation on the Big Island she had stumbled onto evidence of Rusty's theft. And she had spared the thief. It's a wonder she hadn't blown Sammy Bob Pickett's head off, considering what he'd done to her.

I was looking at Rusty's photo when I heard what sounded like light footsteps on the porch. Suddenly the front door pushed open and Kula walked in, dragging his leash. He was huffing and panting, his gold fur was in wild disarray. He looked like he'd been in a chase or a fight. I petted him and felt moisture. His coat was wet.

"Where have you been, boy?" I asked him. "And where's Maile?"

He barked. If only dogs could talk.

I tried to piece together what might have happened. Kula was on leash because Maile had taken him for an evening walk or run. Somehow, the two of them got separated and Kula came home alone. But why would Maile leave Kula on his own? That wasn't like her.

I decided to stay put and wait to see if she returned. It was a dark, moonless night and I didn't expect she'd stay out long. I sat in one of the rattan chairs; Kula walked to the kitchen and took a long drink from his water dish. He came back and lay down beside me, panting a little less than before. Peppah emerged from the kitchen, but kept his distance from Kula. Coconut peeked out from under a rattan chair. Lolo was nowhere in sight. At least she was acting normal.

I waited fifteen minutes. Maile didn't show. By then it was eight o'clock. I'd waited long enough.

"C'mon, Kula," I gently roused him. "Let's go find your master."

The dog got up right away like he knew exactly what I was saying. He led me to my car and jumped in the front seat beside me.

I drove through the dark narrow streets surrounding Maile's cottage. When I didn't find her there, I tried the main street into the valley, East Mānoa Road. Then its side streets. Kula looked anxiously out the passenger window. We were getting nowhere and the night was wearing on.

My cell phone rang. Caller ID said: MAILE BARNES.

"Maile, are you OK?" I asked.

"Now listen up, mate," said the quavering old Aussie voice, "if you want to see this girl again you best bring the gold dog to the Mānoa Chinese Cemetery." It was Abe Scanlon. "Come alone and bring the dog. Even exchange. The dog for the girl."

"Scanlon, you're out of your mind," I said. "The dog's worth nothing to you now that Buckingham's locked up."

"Here . . ." the old man said, "maybe she can talk some sense into you."

"Kai," Maile took the phone. "He thinks he can turn Kula into a fortune. I don't know why, but you're not going to change his mind."

I knew why. Scanlon had built his life around revenge. Now that Buckingham was beyond his reach, his old boss had become desperate and unbalanced. In better times he and Spyder Silva had dog-napped and held Kula, expecting to cash in big. But Maile and I had spoiled that. Now in Scanlon's twisted mind he had a second chance both to cash in on Kula and to strike back at Maile and me.

"Is Silva there?" I asked Maile. "Is he holding you?"

"Yes," she said.

"Does he have his Berretta?"

"Yes."

"So Silva and Scanlon intercepted you while you were out with Kula?"

"Uh-huh."

"And they wanted Kula, but somehow he got away, so they took you instead?"

"Yes." She spoke hurriedly.

"They watched your cottage, waiting for his return. They saw me arrive first, then Kula."

"Y—" Her voice cut off.

Scanlon grabbed the phone. "Chinese cemetery at ten. Bring the dog, mate."

He hung up.

forty-six

I called my attorney friend, Tommy Woo, hoping against hope that he didn't have a gig and he'd drop everything on short notice. Thank God he answered. But before I could get a word in, Tommy said: "Hey, Kai, did you hear the one about the sushi bar on Bishop Street that caters exclusively to lawyers?"

"Can it, Tommy. I need your help and I need it fast."

"It's called Sosumi," he said.

"What?" Once he got rolling there was no stopping him.

"The sushi bar for lawyers is called Sosumi."

"Nice," I said. "Are you free tonight?"

"Yeah. What's up?"

"Can you meet me in my office in fifteen minutes?"

"Well, I'm not dressed . . . but I could throw on something."

"It's an open air gig, so dress appropriately. At the Chinese cemetery in Mānoa. We may have to hike a bit."

"Huh?"

"I'll explain later."

I could have met Tommy in Mānoa and saved the quick trip to my office, but I needed to pick up something there before I faced Silva in the cemetery.

* * *

Tommy, dressed as usual in black, was waiting for me outside the flower shop, which was closed that time of night. Kula was leading me on his leash.

"What's with the dog?" Tommy asked.

"Buckingham," I said.

"Oh, I remember . . ." He brushed back a gray lock.

I let us in through the back entrance. We climbed the stairs to the second floor and found our way to my office door: SURFING DETECTIVE: CONFIDENTIAL INVESTIGATIONS—ALL ISLANDS.

"Have a seat, Tommy," I said as I opened the door. He took my client's chair. Kula led me in and sat next to my desk. I petted him. His coat was nearly dry. His warm fur and renewed calm was reassuring. He seemed to have confidence in me, even if I didn't. I cracked my window overlooking Maunakea Street. The evening bustle of Chinatown's eateries, tourist shops and galleries was winding down. I looked across my desk at Tommy.

"Now here's what we've got," I said. "Maile Barnes is being held hostage by the scums who stole Kula. There's two of them: an old Australian named Abe Scanlon and a local pet thief named Spyder Silva. I've dealt with them before in the Buckingham case. Silva is a sleazy character and the old man is out of his head. He thinks Kula is worth a fortune and he wants to trade Maile for the dog at ten tonight at the Chinese cemetery in Mānoa.

"That's nuts," Tommy said.

"I know, but there it is," I said. "I'm going to approach them in the cemetery alone, as Scanlon specified. I won't have the dog. You will. And since Silva has his Berretta, I'll have my

.357." I pulled the Smith & Wesson from the top drawer of my desk. Tommy was unimpressed.

"What do I do with the dog?" Tommy asked. "I'm a cat person, you know. I don't know much about dogs."

"Don't worry. You don't need to know much about dogs. All you need to do is keep Kula with you and keep him quiet. You two will be in my car, which I'll park a block away from the park. I'm going to tell Scanlon the dog is there with my assistant, but that Scanlon has to release Maile first before I give him the dog. He may not like it. But Scanlon, at his age, is not a physical threat. And I can handle Silva."

"What then?"

"I'm going to take Maile and bring her back to the car."

"And the dog?"

"Kula stays in the car with you. He's not going anywhere."

"You're sure you want to walk into that cemetery alone at night?" Tommy asked.

"Scanlon wants the dog badly. I'm his ticket to gold. He's not going to jeopardize his chances out of the spite he may feel for me. As for Spyder, he'll do what Scanlon tells him to."

"Shouldn't I cover you?"

"With what?"

Tommy pulled from a his black pants a Derringer pistol, bright chrome, and about the size of a cell phone. "It's only .22 calibre," he said, "but it can do the job."

"You never told me you had a firearm, Tommy. I thought it was against your principles."

Tommy adjusted his tortoiseshell glasses. "It's against my principles to get mugged. I'm out late on gigs, in the wee hours, and sometimes not in the best part of town. I'm not about to let somebody whack me on the head and walk off with my keyboard and my car. This little beauty . . ." he caressed the Derringer, "fits right into my pocket. And nobody knows. Well, except you."

"You shouldn't need it tonight. But if you hear a gunshot, you can leave Kula in the car and come running."

"Right on." Tommy grinned.

forty-seven

I closed my office window, locked the dead bolt behind us, and we descended the outside stairs and piled into my Impala— two grown men and a dog. Neither of us said much on the ride from Chinatown to Mānoa. Kula was in back with his head out the window, tail wagging and enjoying the ride. By the time we neared the Chinese cemetery it was almost ten. I parked on East Mānoa Road, a hundred yards down, left Tommy and Kula, and hiked to the cemetery. Scanlon didn't say exactly where I was supposed to meet them, but it's not a huge place and it slopes up the valley, so you can take in the whole view of the place from the lower corner, where I was headed.

But I didn't enter. I stopped and did a quick scan. The cemetery was smack in the middle of the upper Mānoa valley, which ran nearly a mile across. Two small pagodas with jade tile roofs and pillars with Chinese characters in gold stood at the lower and upper entrances. Their marquees said: MANOA CHINESE CEMETERY. The pagoda at the lower entrance, near where I stood, was flanked by royal palms and scrubs that in daylight ranged in color from bright green to flaming red. But at night they were black—like everything else. Behind the pagoda the darkened headstones and plots were carefully tended, showing the Chinese honor and respect for their dead. The cemetery happened to be the oldest and largest of its kind in Hawai'i and during its long history had been the subject of more than a few ghost stories. I couldn't allow my imagination to get started on that. Besides I didn't see any ghosts. Or any sign of Scanlon and Silva and Maile either.

I walked along one edge of the cemetery, staying out of sight and watching for Scanlon and company. The homes bordering the park were huddled close together. Mānoa wasn't Tantalus, and none of the properties resembled palaces on the hill like Wonderview. I scanned a maze of headstones, then reached into my pocket. The cold, hard surface of my Smith & Wesson felt good to the touch. I was glad it was there.

Up the street near the top of the park I spotted a bronze Chevy Tahoe—the same one used in Lehua's kidnapping. Inside were three dim profiles. That was them, all right. The Tahoe was positioned high, in view of the entire cemetery. Scanlon was watching and waiting, expecting me to make the first move. I wouldn't disappoint him.

I backtracked to the lower slope of cemetery and started walking up toward them, in plain view. I wound my way through the headstones, stepping around grave markers to avoid bad luck. I didn't need that. As the land gradually rose, I walked toward the second pagoda at the top of the cemetery. Behind its pillars and jade roof was a huge kukui or candlenut tree whose limbs stretched thirty feet in every direction.

Closing in on the pagoda I looked up again and saw the Tahoe's doors open and Spyder Silva step out wearing his baseball cap, bill pulled down low. Then the old man hobbled out. Maile came next. The two men started walking with her toward the pagoda. She was in her jogging clothes, and her hands were bound behind her. Silva had his grubby mitt on her bare shoulder. I felt like planting a slug between his eyes for that offense alone.

I walked through the pagoda to the kukui tree behind it, stopping under its outstretched limbs. The two men came toward me with Maile. I didn't fear for myself or for Maile because I assumed Scanlon wanted the dog more than he wanted either of us. But suddenly I questioned that assumption. What if wanting the dog was just a ruse? What if Scanlon's real purpose was revenge against the two people who'd ruined his revenge? Already he had Maile. And maybe he thought he'd soon have me. I wished I'd asked Tommy to keep me in sight.

But it was too late. Here came the bald and bent old man hobbling along beside the pet thief, who still had his hand, his left, on Maile. His right was in his pants pocket.

"Where's the dog, mate?" Scanlon said. "You promised to bring him. No dog, no girl."

"I've got the dog," I said. "He's with my assistant within earshot. Once you release Maile there, my assistant will bring the dog."

Scanlon scowled. He didn't like it. "That's not what we agreed on."

"It's the only way I'll do it," I said. "You want the dog—those are my terms. Release Maile first. Otherwise, what guarantee do I have that you won't take them both?"

"What guarantee do we have?" Scanlon said.

"I've got one guarantee, brah!" Hotheaded Silva reached his right hand into his pocket, pulled his Berretta. Bang! He fired it into the ground.

"Idiot," Scanlon scolded him under his breath. Then to me: "You can see that we're armed. And we mean business. You don't want the girl hurt. So you'll produce the dog like you said."

I said nothing. I was recalling my instructions to Tommy. If he heard the gunshot, he'd be on his way.

We had a standoff. Silva kept his gun out, as if he intended to use it. Scanlon whispered in his ear long enough to make me nervous. Almost a minute went by while we all stood there.

Finally, on Scanlon's command, Silva let Maile go. She walked toward me. Her face was expressionless, like a practiced professional. But not for long. Her eyes widened, her mouth gapped, and she said, "Oh, my God!"

Kula came out of the darkness on a dead run. The dog jumped on Silva and knocked him down. Kula started chewing on the pet thief. Silva shrieked and his gun went off again. The dog whelped and rolled on his side. Kula lay motionless.

Silva jumped up, "You fuckah!" he said to me. Then he fired wildly in my direction. I pulled my .357 unloaded two quick rounds into him. He went down again. This time for good.

Maile ran to Kula, who still wasn't moving. "Oh, my God!" she said again.

I subdued Scanlon. Then Tommy showed up with his Derringer pulled.

"Hold this man," I handed off Scanlon.

Tommy showed the old Aussie his Derringer and said, "Stay put."

I ran to Maile, who was standing over Kula. His coat was already bright red. He was wheezing.

"Where did Silva hit him?" I asked her as I unbound her hands.

"He's too bloody." She knelt down beside him. "I can't tell. We've got to get him to an animal hospital—fast."

"I'm on it." I ran down the hill to my car and brought it up. I climbed the curb and pulled into the cemetery, stopping under the kukui tree where Maile still knelt beside Kula.

"How's he doing?" I asked her.

"He's still breathing," Maile said. "I'm worried, Kai."

"Let's get him into the car." Maile and I gently lifted Kula and loaded him in. The upholstery quickly became a bloody mess. I gave Maile the keys, she climbed behind the wheel, and was gone.

I checked on Silva. He lay on his back in a pool of blood. From the holes and expanding stain in his t-shirt, it looked like I'd hit him with both shots in the chest. He had stopped breathing. It didn't appear there was much hope for Silva. There never had been. At the neck of his shirt I could see the border of his tattoo of the coiled cobra and the phrase: KILL 'EM ALL, LET GOD SORT 'EM OUT.

It seemed prophetic.

forty-eight

I dialed 911 and requested police and an ambulance. Silva was dead before either arrived. I was not sad. Whatever made him the way he was, I didn't know. But he had been a scum of the earth, preying on innocent people and their defenseless pets. I remembered what Maile had told me at the beginning of this case: of the many hardened criminals she'd seen during her years with HPD, none were so sick as those who abused animals.

Next I called Frank Fernanadez. The homicide detective showed up about fifteen minutes after three HPD cruisers and the ambulance arrived. Delivering Scanlon to him all neat and tidy would have seemed like a favor under other circumstances, but Silva's body lying only a few feet away with gunshot wounds from my revolver made things a bit more complicated. And I could hardly forget that not long before, Fernandez had liked me for the murders that my client Buckingham had committed.

Before we rode with Fernandez to police headquarters on Beretania Street, I asked Tommy in private: "Did you see Silva shooting at me?"

He nodded.

"Good," I said. "You're my witness. And so is Maile."

"It was self-defense," he said. "No question."

"Why did you let Kula out of the car? I suddenly found myself getting angry at Tommy. "He got shot, man! He's fighting for his life."

"I didn't mean to!" Tommy protested. "When I heard Silva's gun and opened the door to come up and cover you, the dog jumped out. He ran off before I could catch him."

"Sorry, Tommy." I had second thoughts. "It's not your fault. You did the best you could."

"He was flying. Nobody could have stopped him."

"Must be Silva's scent was strong enough for the dog to remember."

"Or maybe Kula picked up Maile's scent or yours?" Tommy shrugged. "I thought golden retrievers were mellow dogs. Yet he attacked Silva."

"Instinct," I said. "Did you hear about the golden on the mainland that fought off a mountain lion to save his human companion? The dog ended up a bloody mess, like Kula, but he survived. I hope Kula does too. Anyway, all I can figure is that he was protecting Maile."

"And you," Tommy said.

* * *

In Fernandez's office, Tommy and I had a long chat with the homicide detective. Frank was a bit torqued that we had not called him before the proposed hostage trade. But Tommy was conveniently and fortunately not only a witness to the events, but also my lawyer. I didn't have to flip open my cell phone to call him. He was already there. And both of our weapons were duly registered in our own names. I had used mine, as Tommy and also Maile would corroborate, in self-defense. We make statements and were released shortly after midnight.

* * *

The first thing I did when I left the station was to call Maile. This time she answered.

"How's Kula?" I asked.

"I hope he's going to make it," she said. "The doc stitched him up and thinks there's a fighting chance he'll recover. He's sedated now and will be in the hospital overnight. I'll go see him first thing tomorrow morning."

"Where are you now?"

"In my cottage. I just got home."

"Ugh . . . Do you have a minute? I thought maybe we could talk—"

"I got your phone message," she said coolly.

"If you'd just let me explain . . ."

She didn't say anything for a moment, then: "OK, I'm too keyed up to sleep."

"Can we talk in person?"

"It's after midnight," she said.

"You're right. It's late . . ."

There was a long pause. Then she said, "Oh, what the heck—"

* * *

I borrowed Tommy's car and drove back to Mānoa wondering how to talk to Maile about the phone call from Madison. Nothing came to mind. It was very late.

When I pulled up the lights were still on inside her cottage. I knocked. Then I heard Maile's distant voice. "The door's open."

I stepped in. No Lolo dashing into Maile's bedroom. No Peppah and Coconut glooming onto me and climbing my leg. Maybe they were asleep?

Maile looked tired and pale. She didn't offer me anything to drink. Or eat. She didn't even say hello. She just said: "I hope Kula's going to be all right."

"Me too,'" I said.

We sat down across from each other. Maile on the rattan couch. Me in a chair. The distance between us felt greater than the few feet that separated our eyes.

She said: "You wanted to talk?"

I took a breath and swallowed hard. "Now about that phone call . . ."

About the Author

Chip Hughes earned a Ph.D. in English at Indiana University and taught American literature, film, writing, and popular fiction at the University of Hawai'i at Mānoa. He left the university in 2008 to write full time. His non-fiction publications include *Beyond The Red Pony: A Reader's Companion to Steinbeck's Complete Short Stories*—also translated into Japanese; *John Steinbeck: A Study of the Short Fiction*; and numerous essays and reviews.

An active member of the Private Eye Writers of America, Chip launched the Surfing Detective mystery series in 2004 with *Murder on Moloka'i*. The second book, *Wipeout!*, followed in 2007. The third, *Kula*, in 2011. Other titles, in various stages of development, include *Murder at Volcano House, Barking Sands,* and the *Maui Masseuse*. The series has been optioned for television and is currently in development. More at http://surfing-detective.com.

Chip lives in Windward O'ahu with his wife and two retrievers. He surfs when time allows.

Made in the USA
Charleston, SC
21 August 2012